anne cassidy

blood
money

Hodder
Children's
Books

a division of Hachette Children's Books

A Catalogue record for this book is available from
the British Library

ISBN 978 0 340 95076 0

Typeset in Baskerville by Avon DataSet Ltd,
Bidford-on-Avon, Warwickshire

Printed in the UK by CPI Bookmarque, Croydon, CR0 4TD

The paper and board in this paperback by Hodder Children's Books
are natural recyclable products made from wood grown in
sustainable forests. The manufacturing processes conform to the
environmental regulations of the country of origin.

Hodder Children's Books
a division of Hachette Children's Books
338 Euston Road
London NW1 3BH
An Hachette UK Company

1

We found the money (all of it in used notes) in an old Nike bag. It was in Mickey Duck's living-room behind a chair that had been tipped over. Bobby kicked it with his foot thinking it was full of old rubbish. Then he went into the kitchen and started opening and closing cupboards. Jack was upstairs stomping around in the bedrooms. I could hear him through the ceiling. I was a sort of lookout; not that we intended to steal anything, or do any damage. We were only being nosy.

Most people wouldn't believe this. They would think that we'd gone into the house to find drugs; to take them down to the youth centre or school and sell them on. A lot of kids did it. But that thought hadn't entered our minds. It was just chance that we were there. We never planned it – though few people would have blamed us if we had.

I should explain. Me – Jaz (short for Janice) – Bobby and Jack were mates. We lived on the edge of a housing estate, all in the same street, Canberra Avenue. The town council had dreamt up an Australian theme so the whole place was usually referred to as 'down under'. Our street was at the nicer end. It bordered the estate and edged on to a park, so a lot of the tenants had bought houses from the council and spent money on them. It was quiet and had trees along the pavement and many of the families had more than one newish car parked outside.

I lived at number 32, Jack at 41 and Bobby further down at 78. We'd all moved into the street during the same year and had started secondary school together. None of us had any brothers or sisters, so we'd been friends on and off ever since. We'd all just finished our GCSEs and were drifting slowly through the long, hot summer waiting for our results and then decisions about colleges.

It was a Friday night and none of us had much money. When this happened we usually headed for the tiny precinct of shops in the middle of the estate. It was where most of the kids gravitated to. There was a chip shop and a tiny supermarket that was also a post office and off-licence. It was ten o'clock in the evening and the heat was lying heavily on the pavement, the night air clammy and thick. There were a few other people around but we were in a threesome chatting among ourselves. Jack had a gas lighter in his hand and was clicking it on and off.

'I wish I had a cigarette,' he said, wistfully.

'Bad idea,' said Bobby.

'It's been two weeks since you had a smoke,' I said. 'Don't give in now!'

Jack shrugged and plonked down on a low brick wall which surrounded a dusty flowerbed. Trevor

Wilkins, a kid we knew, came along on his bike. Without stopping he shouted something about a police raid in Sydney Street. There was hardly a ripple of interest among the other people in the precinct but Jack stood up.

'Let's go,' he said.

'OK,' I agreed. Why not? It was a bit of excitement.

'There might be trouble,' said Bobby.

'Come on, it'll be a laugh,' Jack insisted.

I linked arms with Bobby on one side and Jack on the other and we walked towards Sydney Street. If there was going to be a raid we knew it would most certainly be at Mickey Duck's place. Everyone knew he was the source of drugs and other stolen stuff. When he was flogging carpets and stereos people didn't seem to mind. When it was drugs they did. Either way he wasn't a pleasant character. When the local Neighbourhood Watch group had been round to his house with an anti-drugs petition he'd slammed the door in their faces.

As we were walking along a police car came out of the dark and shot past us. There was no siren or flashing lights but it caused a momentary whoosh of air and then came to a screeching halt a couple of hundred metres up the street. The noise startled me and I grabbed Jack's arm. We looked at each other with surprise. There really was going to be a raid. Me and Jack quickened our steps until we were practically running towards Mickey's house. Bobby followed close behind. By the time we came to a halt another police car had arrived from the opposite direction and the officers had jumped out and run into the house.

We stood watching, gripped by the drama unfolding in front of us. Jack was right close up to the squad car and I was behind. Bobby was by my side, his hand holding my elbow nervously. We were joined by some neighbours and some smaller kids on bikes. There was silence among the crowd as we listened to the sounds of the struggle going on inside the house. There was a lot of shouting and squealing peppered with several different swearwords. It sounded as though there were twenty people in there. In the end four policemen emerged leading out two men. One of them was Mickey Duck, beautifully dressed as ever, his face like thunder. All the way he was swearing and spitting out warnings.

'Watch the suit, watch the suit!'

Behind him was another man. One of Mickey's friends. I'd seen him before but I didn't know his name. He was big, like a bouncer, with a pregnant belly that sat out over his jeans. He wasn't as formally dressed as Mickey but his long hair was held back in a ponytail and I noticed, when he grimaced, that he had two gold front teeth.

The police took each man away in a separate car.

We all stood around for a while. Some of the neighbours were mumbling about how it was 'a good job' and that hopefully they'd put them in prison and 'throw away the key'. Nobody really believed it, though, and bit by bit they drifted off back to their own houses and we were left standing on our own in the street. Trevor, the kid on the bike, sailed past.

'One of them got away!' he said. 'Out the back door and over the garden wall.'

No one ever knew where Trevor got his information from. He just turned up regularly with bulletins which often seemed to come from some fantasy inside his head. Sometimes, like that night, they were true. We watched him disappear up the middle of the street, a car swerving to avoid him, beeping its horn.

We went round the back alley, unfastened the gate and looked into Mickey Duck's back garden. The kitchen door was shut and the place was in total darkness. We looked at each other with disappointment. Then Jack noticed something on the ground. He stepped across the grass and picked it up.

'It's a mobile,' he said.

'Let's see.'

He gave it to me. It was tiny, smaller than most mobiles I had seen. It was heavy and had an expensive feel to it. Bobby took it out of my hand and pressed some of the buttons.

'I know whose this is . . .' Bobby mumbled.

The screen lit up in colour and there was a red and blue logo, an American flag outlined in pixels. I'd seen kids in school with logos on their mobiles. It wasn't owned by a kid, though. We all knew that.

'It's Tommy Young's,' Bobby said. 'I saw him showing this off in the shop last week.'

Tommy Young was one of Mickey's 'associates'. He was as thin as a broom handle and wore black from head to foot every day of the year. He had a thing about America and drove a battered Mustang which he had lovingly restored. He had a lock-up garage on the edge of the estate and was often seen going in or coming out of it, his eyes looking cagily around the street. He wasn't averse to giving any nearby kid a thump, or a couple of quid, depending on the mood he was in.

'Just leave it where we found it,' Jack said, over at the kitchen door. 'Hey look!'

The door swung open. It had been closed but not locked.

'Let's go in,' said Jack.

'I don't think we should,' said Bobby, laying the mobile back on the grass.

We pushed the kitchen door open and stepped into the dark house just to have a look around. Without thinking we flicked the lights on. Anyone who looked could have seen that there were people inside. It didn't matter, though. Because it was Mickey Duck's house, nobody cared. Or perhaps they'd think it was some of his associates, come to tidy up, get rid of stolen gear or flush any drugs down the toilet.

I found the Nike bag behind a chair. I leaned over and picked it up and placed it down on the floor in the middle of the room. I was only mildly interested but Jack and Bobby were rattling round elsewhere so I decided to make myself busy. I thought it might contain CDs or boxes of cigarettes. Mickey always seemed to have plenty of those to sell. I pulled back the zip a few inches and saw what I thought were packets of paper. Puzzled, I squatted down on the floor to unzip it completely. I gasped when I saw what was there. Bundles of notes; twenty, maybe thirty. I held my breath as I lifted one out. It was a few centimetres thick, held with an elastic band. I dropped it and pushed my hand in further. They were all the same. More money than I had ever seen! I stood up with a half-laugh. Then I squatted down again, making a tiny squealing noise in my throat.

Just then Bobby came up behind me.

'Look!'

I said it gleefully, cupping my hands under the money and holding it up for him to see. The sound of Jack's footsteps thumping down the stairs made me drop it, though, and stand up quickly, backing away from the bag.

'We should be going,' Jack said, coming into the room. 'What's that?'

He didn't need an answer. He only looked at it for a second or two then, businesslike, he knelt down and zipped the bag back up. 'Let's get out of here,' he said, quickly. 'In case the police come back.'

Neither me nor Bobby could speak. I don't know

what was going through his mind but I knew that I was doing mental arithmetic, trying to add up the money in my head. There were thousands of pounds in that bag. Jack picked it up and we followed him out into the garden. I don't think any of us had a clue what we were doing. I closed the back door tightly, just as Tommy Young must have done a while before. The three of us stood in the garden, Jack holding the bag, hardly breathing.

'What are we going to do?' I asked.

'Keep it,' said Jack. 'Why not? It's drugs money.'

'You don't know that it's drugs money,' said Bobby.

'Course it is,' Jack replied, with a little laugh. 'How else do you think Mickey Duck gets his money? From all those videos and hairdryers he sells?'

'Ssh . . .' I said, looking around.

The garden was dark and still but I felt exposed. I pulled at Jack's arm, drawing him back towards the shadows of the house. Bobby came as well and we stood in a tight triangle, the bag of money wedged between us. The gardens next door were quiet but I could see light from one of the nearby kitchen windows.

'It's not our money!' Bobby whispered.

'It's not Mickey Duck's either. This is stolen money, Bob. He didn't work for it, he took it. Why should he have it?' Jack reasoned in a hoarse voice.

'I agree with Jack,' I said, even though I had this little finger of worry worming away in my stomach.

'But when he finds out . . . ?' said Bobby, his voice dropping a little.

'He won't find out. Not if we go now. Listen, Bob, this is no one's money. Mickey Duck can't exactly go to the police and say that it's been nicked, can he?'

'But he'll know . . .'

'He'll know *someone's* taken it. He'll think it's someone like him, another dealer or some crooked policeman. He won't know it's us. He wouldn't suspect us – three kids – in a million years.'

'I don't know,' said Bobby.

The sound of a car screeching round a nearby corner made us all look up. It was coming from the street in front of the house.

'We've got to make a decision. We either drop it here and now or we take it and get out of here.'

'I say we *take* it,' I said, and shook Bobby by the arm.

He nodded, looking a bit dazed. Jack didn't wait for any more discussion but walked steadily out of the back garden and Bobby and I followed. We stood in the alleyway with the bag as the sound of car doors slamming and voices came from the street outside.

'Let's go,' Jack whispered, turning in the opposite direction and walking swiftly along the pavement away from Mickey Duck's house and the visitors – whoever they were.

All the way along the road I was thinking about the money. How much was there. How we would hide it. What we would do with it. There were sparks of excitement inside my chest. We had found treasure and part of me wanted to laugh out loud. If I'd known that people would get hurt because of it, I would've cried instead.

2

None of us spoke all the way back from Mickey Duck's house. After a couple of streets we slowed down to walking pace, looking around all the time to make sure we weren't being followed. Jack was hugging the Nike bag, his arms through the handles, squashing it against his chest in an effort to hide it. There was hardly anyone about, just a few kids kicking a football in the dark streets, some women in pairs, coming home from the bingo, their laughter bubbling up and then floating away into the night. We passed by the Peacock pub, its lights bright and cheery, the sound of karaoke coming from inside – a thin, uneven voice then a lot of cheering and clapping. We all seemed to lower our heads and press forward to pass the place quickly. The last thing we wanted was to bump into anybody we knew.

The others were looking long-faced and my initial exhilaration was waning. I found myself tensing at the sound of any car that came up behind us and I jumped when a dog started barking across the street.

What had we done?

Taking a bag of money from someone like Mickey Duck was foolhardy, downright dangerous. If he found

...that we had done it then there would be a price to pay. I hated to think what he'd do to me, Jack and Bobby if he knew that we had his money. I'd heard stories about him over the years: closing people's fingers in car doors, breaking someone's ankle with a spanner, beating up a young lad so that his nose was broken and half his ear had gone. These and other tales had probably been exaggerated, but still, like everyone else, I was fearful of the man. He had a way of standing still as you passed him on the street, picking at fluff on his jacket or trousers while all the time his eyes seemed to be following you along, sizing you up as a customer for his wares or even as a potential trainee dealer. I always ended up feeling a little angry at him, mad even. But like everyone else I avoided him, looking the other way if he was sitting in his red BMW passing envelopes out of the window, taking money nonchalantly, as though he was a regular ice-cream man.

It was too late, though. The money was with us and we could hardly go back and say we'd taken it by mistake. I hurried my steps behind Jack and Bobby. Their profiles were long, Bobby biting at his lip, Jack's face pursed in concentration. We reached his door and I took a last look round. No one had followed us, I was sure.

Jack's parents were out and we went straight upstairs and dumped the Nike bag on the floor.

'Tip it out,' I said, in a half-whisper.

I watched as the bundles thudded on to the carpet and Jack shook the bag roughly in case anything was stuck in the corners. Satisfied that it was empty he dumped the sports bag behind him. Bobby, kneeling on one knee, turned and gave me a look which was a mixture of awe and worry. I glanced up at Jack and locked on his eyes, which were bright and alert and boring into me. We both watched as Bobby sorted the money out until it lay in a line of bundles, possibly twenty-five or more, some thicker than others, all of it in tens and fives, the notes old and wrinkled, some with their corners curling.

'I don't believe this,' I said, to break the silence.

Jack squatted down and ran his hand over the money, the bundles lined up like a set of dominoes.

'We could still take it to the police,' Bobby said, looking at each of us in turn.

'No, not now, we can't,' Jack said, firmly. 'If we hand it in someone will see us, somebody will know. We can't risk Mickey Duck finding out. We made the decision back in that garden. We've got to stick at it. There's no going back.'

'But what will we do with it?' Bobby said, his eyebrows raised, looking sceptical.

'Spend it?' I said.

'On what?'

'I can think of loads of things!' I said, sharply.

'Wait,' Jack said. 'We need to think, we need to take it slowly. Let's count it first, then we'll talk about it.'

I felt immediately annoyed. I hadn't been joking when I'd said that we would spend it. I looked at Bobby, who had started to divide the bundles up, the back of his head nodding slightly as though he was counting or just talking to himself. Opposite him Jack was kneeling down; he'd taken one pack and was flicking through the notes.

'Wait a minute,' I said, stiffly. I didn't like being left out nor did I like being told what to do.

'Jaz, one thing at a time. Let's count it. Then we can see how much we've got and we can make plans! You and Bobby do the fives and I'll do the tens.'

Jack's voice had a sort of finality to it and I decided to let it lie. I sat on the floor, my shoulders heavy with annoyance, and picked up a bundle. While I pulled the elastic band off the notes I thought about how typical the whole scenario was, how absolutely classic it was that Bobby and I should end up taking our orders from Jack.

It had always been the same. Jack Cross, the oldest of the three of us, the most popular and the brightest in school. Always first to get everything: a new bike, skateboard, rollerblades, mobile phone. Did almost no classwork or homework but when it came to getting projects in on time and knowing how to sit exams he had no problems. He had busy parents who always seemed to be off on weekends or holidays. They didn't mind if he didn't get in till late and weren't going to fuss if they caught him smoking or drinking alcohol.

He was his own boss and didn't have to ask permission for anything.

Unlike Bobby. He lived with his mum, who was a nurse; his dad was long gone. Even though I knew her first name I never stopped thinking of her as Mrs Parsons. She had plans for Bobby. He was to go to college and study for A levels and then go on to medical school. It had been decided as far back as I could remember. She had a savings account, Bobby told me, that she had been putting money into since he was little, for his college fees. They didn't have many holidays and didn't even own a car. Their house was immaculately decorated, though, and almost every time you went round there Mrs Parsons was laying down dust sheets ready to repaint one of the rooms. Sometimes Bobby had to help her, or maybe go to the supermarket to help with the shopping. Before his exams he spent a lot of time studying, often rushing back home to swot for an hour with a maths or science tutor. It meant that Bobby was used to doing what other people told him and so when it came to the three of us he always deferred to either me or Jack.

Me? Janice Morgan. I did whatever I felt like. Sometimes I went along with Jack's plans, sometimes I didn't. My school career was a bit like that as well. At some points I picked up my pen, drew a neat line under the title and date and made myself concentrate. At other times I just leant back in my chair and let it all drift over the top of me, wave upon wave of dull information. My results were pretty average, never going below the C-line but hardly ever above. All I needed for college was five passes. What was the point in killing myself to get better grades?

We worked quickly, sitting on Jack's bedroom floor. I was cross-legged, leaning back against the side of the bed. Jack was sitting opposite me, his legs splayed out, taking up more than his fair share of the space. Bobby was beside me, kneeling, hunched over the money. The room itself felt strangely silent. Usually there was constant noise in Jack's house. If it wasn't his mum and dad it was the television from downstairs. Sometimes it was his dad's stereo from along the hallway. Mostly it was us talking or computer games or Jack's CDs. Tonight it was tomb-like. I even found myself breathing quietly.

I had counted my bundles and was flicking casually at the notes, feeling their texture. Bobby was mouthing numbers and Jack was silently counting the notes in front of him, raising his thumb every few seconds to lick it. After a few minutes Bobby sat back and Jack made a sound and slapped the last bundle of money on to the floor.

'Finished!'

Bobby and I told him our totals and he did a quick bit of mental arithmetic.

'That's . . . thirty thousand, six hundred and odd pounds. Thirty thousand pounds.'

Bobby gave a soft whistle. At that moment my

worries about Mickey seemed to evaporate and I looked at the notes and felt this sudden thrill across my chest. It was more money than I had ever imagined spending. No, the buzz inside me was more than that. There was the *audacity* of what we had done, the sheer *recklessness* of it. Like running across the train track, waiting at the other side and feeling the air whipping your face as the train thundered past. Part of me was afraid but part of me was excited.

'What are we going to do with it?' Bobby said.

I was about to repeat my earlier idea about *spending* it but Jack spoke before I could open my mouth.

'Hide it,' he said. 'For six months. Not touch it. Not tell a soul about it. Let the fuss blow over. Then—'

'Six months!' I said.

'Jack's right,' said Bobby. 'We could end up in a real mess because of this. If we're going to keep it we've got to be extra careful.'

I looked crossly at both of them.

'Jaz, we can't spend this money. Not now, not tomorrow, maybe not even in six months' time. We have to lie low, make sure no one links us with it. Mickey Duck will be looking for it. You know that. The only way we're going to get away with this is if we hide the money somewhere and completely forget about it for a long time.'

'But what's the point in having it?' I demanded. 'Why have we gone to the trouble of nicking it, putting ourselves in danger, if we're not going to enjoy it?'

'Because in six months' time we'll all have about ten thousand pounds each and that's more than any of us will get working part-time in Sainsbury's. All we have to do is to be patient.'

After getting used to the sound of 'thirty thousand pounds' the figure 'ten' didn't sound very much.

'And after six months? Won't people notice if we start spending then?'

'That's true,' Bobby said, his face dropping.

'No, we'll divide it up and each keep our own. We can open bank accounts or just keep it hidden and spend it in little bits. Whatever. Mickey Duck will have given up on it by then. We'll be at college. Different people. Who's going to notice if we've got a bit of extra cash on us?'

'Six months!' I sighed.

'It's the only way we'll get to keep it. There is no other way.'

Jack was looking at me with the hint of a frown. As if he was weighing me up, trying to see what I was going to decide ahead of me saying it. His eyes were scanning my face, moving down to my neck and back up again. I'd been under this powerful gaze before and it was making the skin across my chest tingle. I looked down at my hand, my knees and the floor. He was waiting for me to speak. I glanced up at Bobby, who looked less sure than he had before. I pulled myself together. We both had to be positive if we were going to carry Bobby along with us.

'Where are we going to hide it?' I asked.

'That's the easy bit. We'll think of somewhere. The most important thing we've got to do is to agree on total secrecy. That's the hard bit. No one must know about this. No other friends, relatives, no one. Only us. We can't breathe a word of this to anyone. Not only for the six months. For ever.'

I almost laughed at how dramatic Jack sounded. But I knew he was right. It had to be a secret, for all time. If we were going to get away with it.

'We have to be able to trust each other. Completely. We should all swear an oath. Not to tell anyone. Ever,' he said.

'An oath?' said Bobby.

'That's right. Doctors have to do it before they can practise. You know that.'

'Yes, but . . .'

'Is it absolutely necessary?' I said, mockingly.

'It is. If we mean what we say,' Jack said, earnestly.

I knew what he was doing. He was trying to cement us together, to make Bobby feel that he couldn't back out, no matter how uneasy he felt about it.

'I swear not to tell anyone . . .' I said, my voice tapering off at the end, feeling a touch silly.

'I swear to keep this an absolute secret and not talk about it to anyone except for you two,' said Jack, with total sincerity, sounding as though he was about to go and fight for king and country.

We both looked at Bobby. After a moment he shrugged his shoulders.

'OK, I swear not to tell a soul about this money,' he said, in a half-serious voice.

Jack and I avoided looking at each other. I focused on the money and pretended to be tidying it up. I wondered if he was thinking the very same thing as I was. There we were, making Bobby swear to something because we were unsure of his commitment and his loyalty. Three friends promising to be honest and true to each other when I knew and Jack knew that it was all a bit of a farce. How could we be called loyal friends when Jack and I had been lying to Bobby for weeks?

Where was the honesty in that?

3

I should explain. The three of us had been friends for a long time but in the past couple of months Jack and I had stepped out of the triangle and become much more than that. There was probably a list of reasons why it happened. All I know is that we found ourselves alone a lot and a liking for each other's company turned into a desire for something quite different. One minute we were sitting cross-legged on the floor of his bedroom, messing around with an old set of dog-eared cards, and the next he had his arms around me, his fingers running up and down my back, his breath on my neck. We never told Bobby. We had our reasons.

Although we had all been close on and off for almost five years it didn't mean that we were *exclusive* friends. That would have been silly. We all had other friends from time to time. Sometimes we pulled these kids into the group and sometimes they pulled us away from it. Then there were long periods when Jack and Bobby had been closer and I'd felt like the odd one out. They'd spent a lot of time up at the forest, fishing at Heron Lake. Traipsing off for whole days at a time, joining other groups of men or boys, in tents, with chairs and boxes of maggots at their ankles. I wasn't interested in that at all. Jack's football was another thing; he had a season ticket and went with his dad to support West Ham, most home games and some away. As well as that he'd played in the school football team and a local Sunday league. It meant Bobby and I spent a fair bit of time on our own. We often went visiting; sometimes to my gran's or perhaps his cousins who lived at the other end of the tube line – twenty-eight stops in all.

Bobby's absolute best friend was his computer. His mum had bought it for him a couple of years before – expensive, state-of-the-art machine – because she thought it would 'assist' him with his studies and ultimately help him to become a doctor. He used it for schoolwork, I knew that, but mostly he wrote programs that created bizarre screensavers or made up odd tunes that sounded like they'd come straight from some alien spaceship. Mrs Parsons liked it when Bobby was working on his computer. She was never that happy when he was out with me and Jack.

I had had other friends over the years – girls mainly – particularly when my body started to change. That was when I had to shop for bras, tampons and make-up, and then I needed *girls* to talk to. For maybe a year or so Bobby and Jack faded into the background; became just boys who lived on my street and who I occasionally walked to school with.

They went through changes too. Jack shot up and was very thin, his fringe dripping over his eyes and his voice gravelly, sometimes high, sometimes low. It didn't seem to worry him too much. He threw himself into physical activity: football (of course), tennis, cricket, basketball. While I was sitting on the school bench nursing period pains he was running round the school field, driven by a need to always be on the move. He had a sort of girlfriend for a while, Penny Porter. She was sporty, like him, and had this thin, white blonde hair that was always in a ponytail or plait. It lasted a while between them and then seemed to fizzle out overnight.

All Bobby's hormonal changes seemed to happen secretly inside his body. One day he was a kid swapping cards and throwing ten-pence pieces up against the wall, the next he was taller than me, his shoulders were broader and his voice had deepened. He hadn't been ravaged by mood swings or excess perspiration. It was as if adolescence had crept up on him one night and taken possession. One day I noticed him talking to a small dark girl from another class and when I went across to interrupt he blushed and became tongue-tied. After that I was more careful.

By the time we were all in our last year at school the physical upheaval had subsided. Jack had filled out a bit. He kept his fair hair very short and always smelled of soap or deodorant. His lanky look was no longer there, most probably because the rest of us had caught up with him. He was strong, though, his legs and arms muscular and covered with a fine layer of hair. Bobby's dark complexion and hair meant that he often looked as though he needed a shave. He was stocky, with broad shoulders, and looked fit even though he rarely did any physical activity and spent a good deal of time at a desk, either studying or working with his computer. I had filled out a little. The matchstick looks I had when I was a child had gone and now I had a few curves where they mattered. I didn't flaunt it and I still felt most comfortable in casual clothes – jeans, joggers, that sort of thing. My hair was halfway between short and long and had a reddish tint to it.

Although we spent time with other kids we gradually settled back into a threesome. We weren't exactly the same people as before but we still got on together. Jack was a little too confident, always full of plans for the future. He was going to do his A levels, then a gap year, then university. Or he was going to learn to drive, get a car, start up his own courier business (or maybe he would get a motorbike instead). Bobby was the opposite. Always a careful kid, he seemed less sure of himself than ever, checking his pocket half a dozen times to make sure his wallet was there, counting his money carefully, adding up what he'd spent and what he was saving. He loved new clothes even though he could hardly ever afford them. He was always looking in shops, browsing around the racks of designer stuff. If he did get something he looked after it, making sure it was on a hanger or folded up somewhere, clean and ironed. When we were out he always seemed to be looking in a mirror or shop window reflection to check on his appearance.

Me? I just seemed to drift along with the boys. I had a couple of girlfriends who I went out with from time to time but both of them had part-time jobs and money to spend. They started to go places that I couldn't afford and every time I saw them they were dressed up to the nines. It all seemed to take such an effort. It was so much easier to slouch out of my front door and go round to see Jack or Bobby.

In the weeks leading up to the summer exams Bobby became a little withdrawn. He started to study a lot and never seemed to want to come out. Jack and I ended up spending a lot of time on our own. We walked through the estate and headed for the shops at the precinct, talking quietly all the way; we sat by the chip shop watching the world go by; we shared from the same can of drink when the money was short and chatted about Life After School. Trevor Wilkins rode by several times asking, 'Is she your girlfriend?' We rolled our eyes and ignored him.

At some point I must have known. One day, I must have looked at Jack and no longer seen a childhood friend. Maybe it was the way I avoided looking directly into his eyes, embarrassed by his unblinking gaze. Possibly it was the way he started to touch me; a brief hug as we parted, a pat on the back that seemed to turn into a caress, or his attempts to straighten the parting in my hair.

Then there was the afternoon in his bedroom playing with an old pack of cards, laying them out on the carpet.

'I'm worried about Bobby. He's so moody. It's like he's aged ten years,' I said.

'He's just a bit tense,' said Jack. 'He'll get over it.'

'But if he'd just loosen up!'

It was a hot and breezy summer day and the window was open. From the garden below I could hear the sound of a lawnmower and some neighbours shouting to each other across fences.

'He does so much revision! He never gets any fresh air,' I said, continuing my moan.

'He could come to football training on a Thursday. What he needs is a bit of physical activity,' said Jack.

I burst out laughing.

'According to you that's what everyone needs!'

I was holding the cards up in front of me as if I was playing with an opponent and Jack gave me a playful shove.

'You could do with some exercise,' he said, slumping down behind me, his face only centimetres from my back.

When I turned round he put his hands on my shoulders and pulled me towards him. That was the start.

We decided not to tell Bobby. Most people wouldn't believe this but we did it for his own good. We thought that he might feel left out. He might begin to avoid us, thinking that we wanted to be alone all the time. We knew that he was under a lot of pressure from his mum about his exams. We didn't want to upset the threesome for something that might not last, that might only be a bit of fooling around. As soon as the exams were over we were going to tell him.

But we never did.

When the three of us were hanging around together we gave each other little knowing looks and touched hands when Bobby's attention was somewhere else. As time went on we became braver and kissed a couple of times when he'd gone to get a drink or into another room. It became like a game, to see how long we could go on without being found out.

When Jack and I needed to be absolutely *alone* we went up to the forest and sat on the yellow jetty looking out at Heron Lake. We were always careful to make sure no one saw us in case it got back to Bobby. At other times we went to my gran's house, which was empty. I had a key copied so that he and I could meet there. These secret meetings were exciting.

Not for Bobby, though. He knew nothing about it.

4

We agonized about where we could keep the money and then I had a brainwave: my gran's house. No one was living there – it was perfect. The others agreed. We didn't take it over until the next morning. We met at Jack's and tipped it out of the Nike bag and divided it up into three lots. I put some in a leather shoulder bag, Bobby used a rucksack and Jack his sports bag.

'What are we going to do with this?' I said, holding the Nike bag.

'We can get rid of it later,' Jack said. 'We'll dump it in the lake.'

We left his house early, just after nine o'clock. Jack's mum was in the front garden as we walked out. She looked quizzically at her watch, surprised to see us up and out so early.

'We're looking for Saturday jobs,' I said, before she asked.

My gran's house was about fifteen minutes' walk away. We cut across the park, leaving the estate and Mickey Duck's house behind. With every step I took I felt a bigger sense of relief. I wondered if Mickey had returned from the police station. I also remembered, with a slightly queasy feeling, the sound of a car pulling up outside while we ran off from the back garden with the money. Had it been Tommy Young, returning for his mobile phone and the cash? Or had it been someone else, alerted to Mickey Duck's arrest by a neighbour, coming to pick up the Nike bag before the police made any more visits?

I pushed these troublesome thoughts out of my head and noticed that the three of us were walking along in silence, stiffly, like undertakers. Bobby was looking down at the ground as though being careful of every step and Jack was swinging his sports bag from one hand to the other, flexing his wrist, as if his muscle had gone into spasm. He looked like he needed a cigarette.

'Somebody say something,' I said.

'What?' asked Bobby, looking guarded.

'We look like three robots. Anyone would think we had something to hide.'

'You're right,' said Jack, exhaling slowly, as though he was trying to push all of his tension out of his mouth.

Once out of the other side of the park we started to relax.

'You going to football?' Bobby said to Jack.

Jack started to talk about the new football season and Bobby sounded mildly interested. I had a feeling that they were just passing time, trying to pretend that everything was normal. I didn't join in, just cradled my shoulder bag and thought about the night before.

I hadn't slept well at all. When I finally got home

I was buzzing, talking non-stop to my mum and dad who were sitting in the living-room either side of their usual bottle of wine and plate of mixed snacks. The television was on in the corner, although my mum turned the sound down while I told them about the police raid on Mickey Duck's house.

'Not before time,' my dad said, picking his wine glass up by the stem and sniffing in the aroma as though he was a connoisseur.

'He'll be out by tomorrow,' said my mum, her attention drawn back to the television, her finger twitching on the remote, the sound sliding up.

Up in my room I was fidgety. I took my top off, intending to put my nightie on, but instead I just sat down on the bed half-undressed and thought about the events of the evening, my mind jumping back and forth like a film that had been chopped up and stuck back together out of sequence. My emotions danced about. One minute I felt pleased with what we'd done and the next I had this shiver of fear in case we got found out. I kept imagining the money, all those five and ten-pound notes in my lap, ready for me to spend. Then I'd see Mickey Duck's face.

I finally made myself get into bed and turned off the light. I could still hear the television from downstairs, my mum and dad watching some late-night film, no doubt on to their second bottle of wine by then. I lay watching the clock radio, the red numbers blurring in front of me.

Just before I dozed off to sleep I remembered the three of us making the oath and I had this unpleasant, twisted-up feeling inside. All the excitement of the evening had gone flat and I was left with this guilt about Bobby. It wasn't fair that we were keeping something from him, especially in the present circumstances. We should tell him, I thought. How hard could it be? Just sit him down and tell him the truth.

As we walked down my gran's street I felt a sense of ease. This wasn't unusual. It was a walk I had done regularly for most of my life. When I was small I went with my mum or dad. When I got older I skipped along, ahead of them. In the previous few years I'd gone by myself, like an adult, to have tea and chocolate éclairs with Gran and gossip about members of the family and neighbours. I got her keys out of my pocket and held them ready. There were two: a Chubb and a Yale. In the middle of them was the letter K, for Katherine, my gran's name. She had been ill for a long time and was in a nursing home. It hadn't weakened her spirit, though. She refused to sell her house, certain that one day she was going to go home and live there again. Meanwhile, my mum and dad and me (mostly) kept an eye on it for her, making sure everything was locked up and there were no break-ins or squatters.

The house had its usual musty, unlived-in smell and I went straight through into the little kitchen and opened the back door to let the air in.

'I'm starving,' Bobby said, putting his rucksack down

on the kitchen table. 'I'll just go up to the baker's and get something. Anyone else?'

I shrugged my shoulders.

'You could get me a packet of ten,' said Jack, looking sheepish. 'Just to have around. In case I'm desperate.'

He pulled out some money but Bobby waved it away.

'I'm not going to be responsible for you smoking again. I'll get you a doughnut.'

He picked up my gran's house keys and went out into the hall. Moments later we heard the front door close. I was glad we were alone because I wanted to talk about the awkward situation we'd found ourselves in. I didn't get the chance, though. Jack stepped towards me and angled me up against the kitchen door and kissed me.

'Wait . . .' I said, when he pulled back for a breath.

But he kissed me again, his mouth hard against my teeth, his chest tightly up against mine.

'Ssh . . .' he said.

'No.' I pushed him back, my hand gripping on to his T-shirt. 'We've got to tell Bobby, about us.'

'Why? I thought you didn't want to.'

'It's different now!' I found myself whispering, as though Bobby was in the other room, not heading for the shop down the street.

'Why is it different?'

Jack had closed up on me again and was rubbing his hand back and forth across my ribcage.

'The money. The oath . . . All that stuff,' I said, trying

to keep to the subject while my legs were going weak.

'This has got nothing to do with the money.'

'We have to tell him. Today, before we go home . . .'

My voice disappeared as Jack's fingers wormed their way under my T-shirt. I couldn't help it. I closed my eyes and let my head loll back against the door and felt his breath hot on my skin. After what seemed like a long time we pulled apart. It wasn't the right time and we both knew it. My chest was tingling and I felt light-headed, but I pulled myself together and went across to the sink and ran some water. I got a glass from the cupboard and filled it up.

Jack sat down at the kitchen table, his fingers up to his mouth as though he was holding an invisible cigarette. I looked at my watch. Bobby was taking a long time at the baker's.

'We should tell him,' I said.

'If you like,' Jack replied, not really bothered.

I felt miffed for a minute, annoyed at him for not being more interested. Then we heard the sound of the front door opening and Bobby calling out. Seconds later the kitchen door opened.

'Three doughnuts,' he said, dropping a paper bag on to the kitchen table.

'Give us one,' Jack said and pulled the bag towards him.

'You all right?' Bobby said to me. 'You're looking a bit upset.'

'You took your time,' I said, pulling at my T-shirt,

pushing my hair behind my ears and avoiding eye contact with Jack.

'There was a queue,' he explained, shrugging his shoulders.

When we had finished our doughnuts we went upstairs and got out an old suitcase of my gran's that she kept her photographs in. It didn't take us long to empty it and fill it with the money. On the very top we spread out a layer of photographs. The rest, all neatly kept in packets, I put in a drawer by her bed.

'We'll put the suitcase in the loft,' I said.

'What about your mum and dad?' Bobby queried.

'No one goes up there. There aren't any stairs or anything. Anyway, it's mostly me who comes round here these days,' I said, deliberately looking away from Jack.

I got the step ladder out from the cupboard at the top of the stairs and placed it on the landing underneath the loft hatch. Jack went up and opened the hatch. We handed the case up to him.

'Dusty up here,' he said, screwing up his face.

With some puffing he pushed the case into the loft and then closed the hatch. I folded the step ladder and put it back in the cupboard and we went downstairs. We tidied up in the kitchen, closed and locked the back door and were just about to go when Bobby stopped us.

'Hang on.'

Jack and I stood awkwardly in the hall.

'I'm still not happy about this. What we're doing is illegal. I know you say it wasn't Mickey Duck's money to start with, but that still doesn't make it right. Thing is . . . we agreed last night that we would go through with it and I'll stand by that. I'm only doing it because of our friendship, right? Anyone else and I'd back out, but I guess with you two . . . well the three of us . . . You know what I'm saying.'

'Yes . . . look—'

That was the point to tell him. To simply say, '*By the way, Bob, me and Jack have been together for a while, we didn't want to say anything until we were sure . . .*' I absolutely intended to say those words so that everything was out in the open. Trouble was, Bobby kept talking and I couldn't get a word in edgeways.

'— It's always been complete honesty with us three. That's the only way that I think we can see this through. I'll keep it a secret because that's what we agreed to last night.'

'Right,' Jack said, jauntily. 'So that's it, for six months.'

They were both looking at me, waiting for me to speak. I could have confessed then but I didn't.

'Six months,' I repeated, weakly.

'And we don't say a word to anyone,' said Jack.

'Not a soul,' said Bobby, his finger over his lips like a primary school teacher.

We closed and locked my gran's front door and walked away. A few doors along I saw Mrs Reynolds, my gran's old friend. I waved to her and then slumped into silence. I could hear Jack and Bobby's voices talking about some television programme. Jack was striding forward, his step lighter than before, and Bobby looked more at ease, his face breaking into a smile at something Jack had said.

I could have told him, explained about me and Jack, but it hadn't seemed like the right time. I looked at Jack talking animatedly, as if he hadn't a concern in the world. He hadn't thought we should tell Bobby, leastways he didn't seem to care one way or another. Possibly I was worrying about it too much. The main thing was to keep quiet about the money. When the three of us divided it up and we all had our ten thousand pounds would Bobby really care if we had kept a tiny secret from him?

The closer we got to home the better I began to feel. The money was hidden and didn't need to be moved for the foreseeable future. All we had to do was keep quiet. No one could link us with it.

There was nothing to worry about.

Except that when we came out of the park and back into Canberra Avenue the first person we saw was Trevor Wilkins riding around on his bike. Parked behind him was a red BMW and as we walked closer a man got out of it, dressed in a light grey suit. He was waving at us as though we were long-lost friends.

It was Mickey Duck.

5

'Where you lot been?' Mickey said when we got close enough.

He was leaning against the BMW, talking as though he knew us, as if we were acquaintances of his, people he nodded at or spoke to every day. Trevor cycled up to him and stood still, balancing the bike between his legs.

'What's up?' I said, giving a nervous half-smile.

I don't think any of us had ever really spoken to Mickey Duck. He'd arrived on the estate a couple of years before and moved into Sydney Street with a woman and her children. He was younger than her, in his early thirties, and it took a while for his reputation to grow. Everyone knew him as Mickey Duck but his real name was Donald Michaels. The nickname came from schooldays and it seems he'd been happy enough to let it stick. The woman left him after a while and he stayed on in the house and became a sort of institution; the local crook, someone who always had some scan going on. When the drugs came along people started to avoid him.

We saw him around, of course, and he occasionally glanced our way. We were a bunch of teenagers among many that he came across in his day-to-day life. We didn't do drugs and we didn't buy any of the gear he sold around the estate. We had no real contact with the man and yet there he was talking to us as though he knew who we were. It gave me a choppy feeling in my guts; as though he had been watching us; as though he knew everything.

'I been waiting to have a chat. Trevor here says you were in my street last night when I had that little bit of trouble.'

'We were around,' Jack said, his voice light and easy.

'I wanted a quiet word,' he said, and edged backwards towards his car.

'We didn't see anything,' Bobby blurted out.

I felt as though a stone had just surfaced in my stomach. Another few seconds and Bobby would confess the lot. I put my hand up and linked his arm, my fingers gripping his skin.

'Except you and your mate being carted off,' Jack said, trying to sound like he was making a joke.

'A little misunderstanding with Her Majesty's constabulary,' Mickey Duck came back. 'Anyway, that's not what I wanted to chat about. Why don't you step inside my office?' He pointed at the car.

I felt Bobby tense, holding back, and I caught Jack's eye. None of us wanted to get into the red BMW but Mickey Duck was standing, holding the back door open, and it would have been a stupid thing to do to refuse him. I took the lead.

'I can't stay long. If my mum sees me I'm in trouble,'
I said.

I stepped into the car and slid across the leather
seat. Jack edged Bobby into the middle, following him
in. Mickey closed the door and walked round the front
of the car. I watched as he took his wallet out of his
inside jacket pocket and pulled out a note, possibly a
fiver, and gave it to Trevor.

He got into the driver's seat, leant over to the glove
compartment and drew out a small duster. I shot a
quick look at Jack, who gave me a reassuring nod.
I didn't look at Bobby but I could feel him, like a
dead weight on the seat beside me. Mickey Duck
was cleaning the dashboard, rubbing in little circles.
He didn't seem to be in much of a hurry. After a
few seconds he turned to face us. He took a deep
breath.

'Here's the problem,' he said, and I found myself
pushing my leg close to Bobby's. 'When Billy Ross
and me went to help the police with their *enquiries*
somebody broke into my house.'

He stopped and I remembered the other man with
the big stomach and the gold teeth. I wondered where
he was.

'It wasn't us!' Jack said, his voice strong with a hint
of indignation.

'Do I look like I'm accusing you?'

There was a steely tone to Mickey Duck's voice.

'No, but . . .'

'All I'm asking is if you'd seen anyone . . . hanging around my place. Trevor said you went round the back.'

Mickey Duck replaced the duster in the glove compartment and snapped it shut. Then he turned round and rested his hand on the back of the driver's seat. I noticed his watch then, a wafer-thin gold face with no numbers on it, just the hands pointing at the hour and the minutes. It was the sort of watch that cost an awful lot of money.

'Just other neighbours,' Jack said.

'And Trevor,' I added, not wanting to stay completely silent.

'But no one else?' he asked, looking from Jack to me and then back again.

'Nope,' said Jack.

'Only, I'd be, what you call, *unhappy*, if I thought you had seen anyone and kept quiet about it.'

'We wouldn't,' I said.

He started to nod his head and I saw, through the windscreen, the other man, Billy Ross, walking towards us. Mickey Duck had seen him as well and was opening the electric window, waiting for him to level with the car.

I made hand signals to Jack. 'We'll be off,' he said, and started to fiddle with the door handle.

Mickey Duck turned and looked almost surprised to see that we were still there. Then his eyes rested on Bobby, who hadn't said a single word all the time we'd been in the car.

'What's wrong with him?' he asked.

'Nothing,' said Jack, opening the door. He was about to get out of the car when Bobby suddenly piped up.

'I saw Tommy Young coming out of your back gate.'

We both looked at him with dismay. Why did he have to say that? We were almost out of the car. We had just about got through the interrogation, mild as it had been.

'Tommy Young?' Mickey Duck said, looking sharply. 'Why didn't you say so before?'

Billy Ross had reached the car and was leaning down, looking into the back seat, his eyes travelling from side to side, looking us over.

'We thought,' Jack said, with a hint of hesitation, 'that Tommy Young was with you. We thought you knew he was there.'

'Not that night,' Mickey Duck murmured, and turned his head away from us. I caught a knowing glance between him and Billy Ross, whose head was almost in the driver's seat alongside his boss.

I made a face at Jack to get out.

'He was just leaving, walking away down the alley at the back,' Bobby carried on.

I pinched his arm and nudged him to move over. Jack was out of the car by this time, standing on the road, holding the door.

'Was he carrying anything?' Mickey Duck said.

'No,' I said firmly, hoping that my voice would cover anything that Bobby might say. 'Not that I could see.'

Then I pushed Bobby and the two of us slid along the seat and got out of the car. We stood uncertainly in the street, not knowing whether we had been dismissed or not. Billy Ross lumbered round to the passenger's side and opened the door. Before getting in he gave us a long look, his gaze moving from Jack to Bobby and then to me. When the engine started he dragged his eyes away and got into the car. The BMW roared up the street and turned the corner. Only then did I feel my legs quivering. I looked at Bobby and felt my temper rise.

'What did you have to say that for?' I demanded.

'Not here,' said Jack, looking at a couple of neighbours who had come out on to the street.

'Come into mine,' said Bobby, his voice low and uncertain.

We followed him into his house. Thankfully Mrs Parsons was out and the place was empty. As we went into the kitchen Jack's ring tone sounded and he got his mobile out to answer it, walking back into the hallway.

'All you had to do was to act natural!' I hissed at Bobby. 'You didn't have to tell him anything.'

'Why not? Tommy Young was there. Why should we lie?'

Bobby was fidgeting, brushing down his T-shirt, looking sheepish.

'We don't know Tommy Young was there. We just saw his mobile!'

'What does it matter? It takes the focus off us!'

'There never was any *focus* on us!'

I was spitting my words out, furious that Bobby couldn't see that Mickey Duck was just asking us, the way he had no doubt asked Trevor. We hadn't needed to say a thing. Most probably he would have forgotten all about us, but now that we'd mentioned Tommy Young he would be back for more, I was sure.

I stamped out into the hall to Jack. He was talking into his phone, his voice chirpy and light.

'Do you want some tea?' Bobby shouted, in a conciliatory voice.

I didn't answer.

Bobby was making tea and Jack was talking on his mobile. How normal everything seemed. As if the three of us weren't under pressure. As if it was just another ordinary day. We hadn't just hidden thirty thousand pounds in my gran's loft. We hadn't just told a bucketful of lies to the local hard man.

Jack and I were out of Bobby's line of vision and he put his arm around me, holding me in a playful neck lock.

'My dad's got the new season tickets!' he whispered.

The person on the other end was still talking and Jack put his mouth on to my neck and licked my skin. I let myself relax, my shoulders rippling with delight. I nuzzled into his face.

'I've got some biscuits.'

Bobby's voice came along the hall at the same time as his footsteps on the wooden floor. We jumped apart, not sure if he'd seen us. Jack was nodding exaggeratedly into his phone and I stood looking in the hall mirror, pretending to fix my hair.

'What sort?' I said, coughing to cover my embarrassment.

'Digestives,' Bobby replied, his expression hard to read. In his hand was an oriental biscuit tin with swirling patterns on it.

Jack nodded, giving a thumbs-up sign, and then continued to talk loudly about football.

'Only if they're chocolate,' I said, wiping away Jack's kiss from my neck.

6

Jack and I were in his bedroom a week later when I noticed the Nike bag in the corner behind his laundry basket.

'I thought you said you'd get rid of that,' I said, slightly shaken to see it lying there, looking innocent, as though the only thing it had ever carried was a football kit.

Jack was lying flat on his bed listening to music and he didn't hear me at first. He sat up, stretching his arms out so that I could hear his bones creak. His shirt was undone (my fault) and he was concentrating, doing each button up.

'The money bag. I thought you were going to dump it.'

'I was. I am. It's just that since talking to Mickey Duck I don't want to be caught with it. I'll give it another couple of days then take it up to the lake and chuck it in.'

He reached over to the bedside table and picked up a packet of chewing gum. Giving up smoking was getting him down and he was using gum to keep his mind off it. I liked it. He tasted of spearmint.

'But what if someone sees it?' I said weakly.

'Who? My mum and dad don't come in here. Anyway, what would they think if they did? It's just a sports bag. I've got a couple more under the bed somewhere.'

There was no answer to be made. Jack's words were perfectly sensible, even if I did feel uncomfortable every time I looked at the bag. He put his hand out and I climbed back on to the bed and lay down beside him.

'Bobby should be back from his cousins' soon,' he said, looking at his watch.

'Don't forget it's twenty-eight stops on the Central line.'

He didn't answer and I just lay in the crook of his arm. In the week since we had found the money things had been up and down. The three of us had spent a lot of time together, showing our faces all over the estate. Jack had said this was the right thing to do. Any suggestion of us avoiding our usual haunts or feeling awkward if we passed by Mickey Duck and his mates would look suspicious. We had to act unconcerned, as though everything was ordinary.

This meant that Bobby was with us virtually every moment, which was getting on my nerves. When we weren't out somewhere, showing ourselves to anyone who cared to see, we were in one of our houses and Bobby was there, beside us, in front of the telly or round the kitchen table or even playing cards, something he hated doing except on his computer.

It meant that Jack and I had no real time alone, and when the three of us were together it seemed as though I ended up talking to Bobby, reassuring him about the money.

On top of that, Bobby had lost his cash card and was constantly worried that someone might be using it. He got me and Jack to go to the bank with him, so that he could find out for sure what his balance was. It seemed as though he couldn't do a single thing on his own. I hardly ever got to talk to Jack and he took to spending a lot of time text-messaging on his mobile. The football season was starting, he said, and he was finding out team news and scores of friendly matches.

After the initial excitement of taking the money it had all become very dull. So when Bobby said he had to go and see his cousins in west London I felt like shouting 'Hurrah!'. It gave Jack and I a big chunk of the day to be on our own and we'd made the most of it. Without giving it much thought we'd slipped into talking about the money.

'I'm getting a car,' Jack said. 'I'll buy one privately with cash. Most people will think I've bought it from a dealer's and I'm paying it off monthly. That way no one will be suspicious.'

I didn't comment. He would change his mind over the coming months, I was sure.

'What about you?' he asked.

'Dunno. Clothes? A new mobile? Not much else straight away. Put some of it in a savings account, keep some of it under the floorboards, maybe have a holiday. I won't have any trouble spending it, don't you worry.'

'You could buy some new clothes,' he said, looking me up and down with just a hint of criticism.

I looked down at what I was wearing. An oldish T-shirt and jeans. Both clean, although the T-shirt hadn't been ironed.

'What's wrong with my clothes?' I demanded, half joking.

'Nothing,' said Jack. 'It's just that you've got a nice body. You should show it off more often.'

'Oh, yeah,' I said. 'I would have thought you'd like my clothes best when I wasn't wearing them.'

He gave a fake laugh and pinned me down, his body draped heavily over mine. Then he looked at me for a moment and gave me a light kiss, his lips just brushing mine, his tongue just edging past my teeth. I felt this rush in my chest, my breasts tingling with pleasure. Then we lay on his bed for a while, me moving one way and him the other, his hips pushing into mine. Underneath, I could feel his duvet becoming entangled in my legs, and in my ears I could feel his breath strong and loud. After a while we both stopped, pulled ourselves apart and sat up. My heart was galloping and my skin was tingling. He looked hot and distracted and slightly pained.

Most people wouldn't believe that we could just stop like that. But I'd told Jack when we started that I didn't want to go the whole way. I knew of several teenagers who had got pregnant and I had no intention of being one of them. On top of that there were the diseases that could be passed on. I didn't even want to think about those. I could have gone to the doctor and got some contraception, but the questions and the thought of an examination put me off; it was all too embarrassing. Jack had bought some condoms but I didn't like the idea of them: slimy, horrible things. So we usually messed around for a while and stopped at a certain point, pulling back and panting like a couple of boxers at the end of a round.

We decided to go out to the precinct. Jack was intending to buy a packet of ten cigarettes – just for emergencies, he said. I went along planning to talk him out of it.

Along the way we saw Bobby walking towards us down the road, coming from the direction of the tube station. From a distance he looked like a different lad. He was striding along and looking as though he was bursting with confidence. As he got closer I could see he was carrying a couple of plastic bags.

'All right?' he said when we got up to him.

I nodded and focused on the stuff he was carrying. A bag in each hand, sports logos on the outside.

'New clothes?' I asked.

'My uncle gave me some money,' he said, looking pleased with himself.

I was about to delve into his bag and have a look

when I heard a car screech around the corner. It was a sound that set my teeth on edge and I looked up to see an old white Mustang parked untidily. Out of the passenger's seat jumped Tommy Young, in a black T-shirt and jeans, his face paler than usual, striding across the street in our direction.

'*Oi!*' he shouted.

We closed up and stood very still. I found myself clenching my fists, wondering what was coming next. I didn't have long to wait because he walked straight up to Bobby, gripped his shoulder with one hand and pushed him hard against a brick wall. Bobby dropped his bags, his hands going up to Tommy Young's arm to try to loosen his hold. Jack stepped sideways and so did I. We both stood absolutely still for a few seconds, neither of us doing a thing, poor Bobby pinned up against the wall, his face stricken.

'You been talking to Mickey Duck about me?'

He was shouting the words into Bobby's face, his voice strained and cracking. Jack seemed to pull himself together and put his hand up on to Tommy Young's arm.

'Leave him alone . . .' he said, weakly. 'You can't . . .'

'Push off. This has got nothing to do with you!' Tommy Young shouted, his face turned away from Bobby for a moment.

'He's my mate,' Jack said, his voice louder, his shoulders squared.

But he was no match for Tommy Young, who

dropped his hold on Bobby and turned to Jack, giving him a shove that sent him flying along the pavement. Jack ended up sprawled on the ground, looking up at Tommy who stood threateningly over him.

'You keep out of my way. Don't talk to anyone about me because it's none of your business, right?'

Then he turned back to Bobby, giving me a dismissive glance. He put the flat of his hand in the middle of Bobby's chest and pinned him up against a lamppost. I bent down and picked up Bobby's bags, feeling weak-headed and hopelessly inadequate. Jack was easing himself off the pavement and I could hear Tommy's voice hissing at Bobby, telling him to keep his mouth shut.

A couple of people had come out of their houses by then and Tommy Young seemed to notice. He stepped back, taking his hand from Bobby's chest. He looked at us with loathing and then walked off back to the car. Bobby wavered a moment, as though he might topple over. I saw him grab the lamppost and turned to see Jack holding his hip and grimacing with pain as he went sheepishly to lean on a nearby wall.

Tommy Young got into the Mustang, revved it up loudly and drove off.

The three of us were in a state of shock, me holding the clothes bags, Bobby clinging to the lamppost and Jack looking waxy, his hands gripping on to the bricks. Jack and Bobby had been hurt and I was shaken up so it took a long time for anyone to say anything. Finally,

Jack spoke, his voice croaky, sounding as if he was on the edge of tears.

'I won't forget that bastard,' he said.

And he didn't.

7

That night I had to go to my gran's house. I was going to pick up some sewing and a watch that she'd asked my mum to get. I didn't mind going, in fact I was glad to have something to do that distanced me from the estate.

My gran had had a stroke a year or so before. It was me who'd found her the following morning, sitting in her special TV chair, her glasses lopsided on her face, the cup of tea she had been drinking tipped over on to the carpet. I'd knocked for a few minutes and when she hadn't opened the door I'd used our spare key and let myself in.

I'd been surprised to see her watching television in the morning because it wasn't something she ever did. The lamps were on in the living-room, as well as the hallway lights. I stopped when I saw the cup and saucer lying on the floor beside her chair.

'Gran, what have you done?'

I'd said it in a jokey way and squatted down to pick them up. But the cup and the damp stain were stone cold. I looked at her then, her glasses all crooked, one side of her face drawn down. She was awake and disorientated and said something to me. 'What?' I'd 'said, still not realizing what had happened, and she spoke again, her words incomprehensible, a different language. I took her hands and they were icy. It dawned on me slowly. She'd been sitting there all night long. I called my mum and the ambulance and ran upstairs to get a blanket, to keep her warm.

My mum went with Gran to the hospital and I was left to clear up, scrubbing the carpet hard to get rid of the tea stain. Then I noticed that the seat she'd been sitting on was also damp and I felt my cheeks flush with embarrassment for her. Her glasses were down the side of the cushion, they'd come off completely when the ambulance crew had picked her up. I held them in my hand and felt my throat tighten up.

She'd stayed in hospital for weeks and even tried coming home for a while. It hadn't worked out, though; she'd needed a lot of care. That was when everyone (my mum and dad) decided she should go into the nursing home. 'Just for a while,' they'd said, but she'd been there ever since.

'You'll see me sitting in my own front room, in my TV chair again,' she'd said to me. 'You mark my words.'

She often said that. *You mark my words.* As though she was afraid that I wasn't really paying attention. But it was hard to imagine Gran back to normal, in her TV chair, a cup of tea in her hand, watching her favourite programmes.

I left home at about seven. Normally I would have asked Jack to go with me but he was going to some football training. Anyway, after our experience with Tommy Young in the afternoon I didn't feel very sociable, and I don't think he did either.

Bobby had been badly shaken by it and we walked up to his house with him, trying to calm him down. Jack, even though he was trembling with indignation, seemed to find just the right words.

'Just stay calm. The very fact that he's come after us for grassing him to Mickey Duck means that he doesn't suspect us. No one suspects us. We're just a few irritating teenagers who have been blabbing. Absolutely no one thinks we've got the money.'

Bobby clutched his shopping bags, looking sick and saying nothing, as though he didn't trust himself.

'Jack's right,' I reassured. 'Nobody thinks we have the money.'

'It's all right for you!' Bobby said with sudden anger. 'Nobody pushed you around!'

He was right. It was a male thing and I had come out of it physically unscathed, although even I had been frightened by Tommy Young's threatened violence. I didn't answer him and he went indoors. Jack said something about seeing him the next day and Bobby mumbled some reply. Then his front door shut.

On the way to my gran's house I tried to put the afternoon out of my mind. I made myself think about the future instead. In less than three weeks' time Jack, Bobby and I were starting at the same sixth-form college (always assuming we got the exam results we needed). It was something we'd all longed for. Leaving school behind; no more uniform, no more moany teachers, smelly school dining-rooms, classrooms that were too hot in the summer and too cold in the winter. Most of all no more being treated like a kid, spoken to as though we were five years old. How we'd all longed to put that behind us and now it was really happening.

The college was only about ten years old: new buildings, big computer suite, a choice of two canteens. We could wear our own clothes, smoke outside the building if we wanted, choose what we wanted to do with our free periods. We were to address the staff by their first names, no more stuffy 'Sir' or 'Miss'.

And on top of it all, in six months' time, the three of us would have serious money to spend. My mood was lifting and I found myself bouncing along the pavement. I passed by my gran's old neighbour, Mrs Reynolds, and chatted to her for a minute. By the time I opened Gran's front door and turned the hall light on I'd almost forgotten the events of the afternoon.

The house always felt bigger when I was on my own. The quiet inside was churchlike and I often found myself tiptoeing around, closing the doors quietly, not clearing my throat too loudly in case I disturbed anything. After shutting the front door I walked upstairs to my gran's bedroom. On the landing I couldn't help but glance upwards at the loft hatch. After the events of the afternoon it gave me an uncomfortable feeling. While I was there, so close to the *actual* money, I felt curiously vulnerable. On the estate, fifteen minutes' walk away, I could almost believe that the three of us knew nothing about it.

I went into the main bedroom and looked at my gran's single bed, still made up even though it had been empty for a long time. I walked across and pulled the covers back to give it an airing. There was a satin eiderdown covered with a crocheted multicoloured blanket. Underneath was a fluffy pink blanket. No duvet for my gran. 'I can't be having with all those modern things,' she'd said, firmly. Next to it, on a table, was a tiny silver alarm clock that I had bought for her one Christmas. It hadn't been wound up for a long time and the hands had stopped at a quarter to four.

I knelt down in front of her wardrobe and pulled out her sewing box. It was a square basket full of sewing paraphernalia. I flipped the lid up and sorted through to find some of her embroidery samples, some needles and a reel of thread.

The jewellery box was in the bottom of her wardrobe. I got it out and put it on top of the dressing table. When I lifted the lid music started to play and the small figure of a ballerina began to turn round slowly. I was taken aback for a few moments and sat down on the bed to watch it.

How old had I been when I last opened that box? Only a little girl, four or five maybe; most certainly before I'd gone to school. Watching it was giving me the oddest feeling. The tune was from *Swan Lake* and it was like a tinkly piano, just one note at a time as the figure of the ballerina pirouetted on her pedestal. My mum had worked then and my gran looked after me in the afternoons. We used to sit here in her room, together. She'd be on the bed, her legs crossed at the ankles, a heavy glass ashtray placed on her lap and in her fingers one cigarette after another, the ash falling in chunks. I would be sorting through the dressing-up drawer, trying things on, looking in the mirror, walking up and down the room to show off my new outfit. Dresses that swamped me, high heels that made me list forward, shawls that wrapped round me like a sari, hats that covered my head and sometimes my eyes. The jewellery was always the best bit: pearls that had to double up around my small neck, earrings that clipped hungrily on to my lobes, bracelets that jangled together, weighing my arms down. My gran always told me how beautiful I looked. 'You'll be a model one day, you mark my words,' she'd say, pointing at me with her cigarette.

I picked up her watch and put it with the embroidery. Then I looked away from the dancing figure, around the room, and my eyes settled on the silly old covers on the bed, the abandoned sewing basket, the bedside cabinet where the clock had stopped at quarter to four and I felt this ache in my chest. I pictured my gran the last time I had seen her. She'd been sitting in a chair in the TV-room of the nursing home, too far away from the set to hear the programme, waving me goodbye as I left to go home.

I cleared my throat and snapped down the lid of the jewellery box, silencing the music. I sat there quietly for a few moments then I picked up my gran's things, pulled her bedcovers back up and left the room.

On the landing I looked up at the loft hatch and felt this sense of foreboding. The experience with Tommy Young had unsettled me just as much as the other two. But when it came down to it nothing had actually happened. We were in the clear. Nobody knew we had the money. I made myself look away, to the walls covered in my gran's pictures, to the carpet with its blousy floral design, to the other room doors: the second bedroom, the bathroom, the separate toilet.

I noticed the ladder then. It was leaning against the wall underneath one of gran's pictures. Two kittens peeking out of a paper bag. I walked up to it, frowning. I had to think hard. I was sure I'd put the step ladder back in the cupboard. I remembered Jack coming down from the loft covered in dust and then I folded the ladder up and put it away. Except that it wasn't in the cupboard now. It had been moved. By whom? Had my mum been to the house without me knowing?

At that moment a completely unexpected thought popped into my head. *Had Jack or Bobby been to the house without telling me?* But no, that was silly. Why would they? In any case Bobby didn't even have a key.

I walked down the stairs trying to shrug off an unpleasant sensation. Perhaps I was mistaken. In the excitement of the day I hadn't put the ladder back. Or, when we went downstairs, Jack or Bobby had gone back up and moved it for some reason. I shook my head. I knew that they hadn't. It must mean that my mum had made a visit to my gran's for some reason.

I turned off the lights and locked the front door. The light was fading as I walked down my gran's street and back into the park. There were still groups of kids playing football even though it was almost too dark to see the ball. The security men were hovering round the exits waiting to lock up and I quickened my pace, reaching the other end of the park and Canberra Avenue just as several groups of children and teenagers were being escorted out of the gate.

My mum was at home, sitting in her usual chair with a glass of red wine by her side. The telly was on, the volume higher than it needed to be. I had to speak loudly before she realized that I had come in.

'You got your gran's stuff,' she said, nodding towards the watch and the embroidery that I'd put on the coffee table.

'Have you been to gran's lately?' I blurted out.

But she'd stopped listening to me, her eyes drawn back to the television.

'Mum.' I squatted down beside her chair. 'Did you pop into Gran's house this week?'

'No,' she said. 'Why do you ask?'

I stood up without answering, my stomach heavy, my shoulders dipping.

'No reason,' I said, unhappily.

8

I never got a chance to ask Jack about the ladder. The next morning was chaos. It started when there was a loud banging on my door. I opened one eye and looked at the clock. It was only just gone eight. My dad was already at work and I could hear my mum in the shower so I had to lever myself out of bed, put on my dressing gown and answer the door in my bare feet. Bobby charged past me, agitated. He had old jogging trousers on and a wrinkled T-shirt. He looked quite unlike his usual self.

'Tommy Young's lock-up has been burnt out,' he said.

I looked at him curiously. It took me a minute to register what he was saying. *Tommy Young's lock-up.*

'Come in the kitchen,' I said, and walked along the hall. 'I'll make some tea.'

'Not now. We need to go and see what's happened!'

'Burned out? I don't understand,' I said, licking my dry lips.

'I went to tell Jack but he's not there. This could be bad. I don't even know whether he was in it at the time.'

He was sounding mildly hysterical.

'Wait here,' I said. 'I'll get dressed.'

I was still sleepy, with a furry taste in my mouth, but I realized then what Bobby was saying. I pulled on some jeans and a top and put my trainers on my bare feet. I didn't even bother to comb my hair, I just ran my fingers through it and went back downstairs. A week or so before, Bobby had told Mickey Duck that he'd seen Tommy Young outside his house on the night the money was stolen (when, strictly speaking, he hadn't). Now Tommy Young's lock-up garage had been set on fire. I called goodbye to my mum and then we left.

As we walked along Bobby told me how he'd found out. He'd gone to the precinct shop for some milk and been passed by the fire engine, its lights flashing. Someone – surprisingly not Trevor Wilkins – had said that one of the lock-ups had been set on fire by Mickey Duck. Bobby had walked towards the commotion and found a load of people standing round in their night clothes looking at thick black smoke pouring from the garage. Tommy Young wasn't there but it had definitely been his garage because people were talking about a falling out between him and Mickey.

Bobby, the pint of milk still in his hand, had rushed home.

'This is probably nothing to do with what you said to Mickey Duck,' I said, thinking the opposite. A mildly nauseous feeling was forming inside my stomach.

Whether that was to do with Tommy Young or the fact that I hadn't had any breakfast, I wasn't sure.

As we walked past the precinct shops I could see the smoke above the rooftops, grey and wispy, looking half-hearted. We turned the corner and saw the little crowd of people still hanging around the edges of the fire engine. A couple of the firemen were rolling up hoses but the rest were just milling around talking to the neighbours. One was squatting down, chatting to a couple of kids, and another was sharing a joke with a lady in a short nightie.

There was no ambulance and I breathed more easily. No one, it seemed, had been hurt. We walked closer and looked at the garage door. It was one of those metal ones with a handle in the middle. It was blackened and looked like the bottom of a pot that had been left on the stove too long. The corners had curled a little and there was steam rising off it where it had been sprayed with water. The door had been lifted upwards and was at an angle to the garage opening, no doubt so that the firemen could check whether anyone was in there or not. Their lighthearted manner suggested that no one had been. I couldn't see into the garage very clearly but it looked black and sooty and the air in front of it seemed to waver with heat.

'Where's Tommy Young?' I said to a pregnant woman beside me.

'He's gone. Someone saw the Mustang drive

off early,' she answered, rubbing her hand over an enormous stomach.

'Oh,' I said, nonchalantly. I nudged Bobby and we turned to walk away.

'That's it,' I said. 'No one's been hurt. It could have been an accident. No one knows for sure. It's nothing to do with us.'

'But where is Tommy Young?' Bobby said, tucking his T-shirt into the waistband of his jogging trousers.

'After the way he treated us yesterday he could be at the bottom of the lake for all I care.'

Bobby didn't say anything and I could tell he was deeply uneasy. Out of the corner of my eye I could see him smoothing out the T-shirt, trying to flatten the wrinkles, his expression grim. It irritated me and I wanted to snap at him and tell him to pull himself together. But I was still quite tired and I needed a cup of tea so I didn't bother. We walked quietly on until we came to Canberra Avenue and were just about to turn into it when I heard the beep of a car horn. The red BMW was down a side street and I could see Mickey Duck standing at the driver's door beckoning for us to walk over.

'Relax,' I hissed through a smile and hoped Bobby would lighten up.

In a moment we were there at his side. Billy Ross was in the passenger seat, wearing a pair of pebble sunglasses even though there was no sun. He was reading a newspaper and looked up at us now and then.

'My good friends,' said Mickey Duck, a beaming smile on his face.

'What's up?' I said and wished that Bobby would speak.

'Just been sorting a few things out and wanted to thank you youngsters for your help.'

He said the word 'youngsters' in such a way that it sounded insulting. I didn't answer.

'Here's what I found in a mate's garage.'

He pointed to the back seat of his car and I took a couple of steps so that I could look inside. I swallowed a couple of times as I peered through the dusty windows, not believing what I was seeing. I turned to Bobby and he looked shaken. I looked back and there it was. The Nike bag. The one we had stolen from his house.

'What's that?' I said, trying to look bored and not bothered.

'It's that item I was looking for. Well, it's the bag that held the item anyway. All I needed was a little nudge in the right direction and your friend here helped me along. So I wanted to give you this.'

I dragged my eyes away from the bag in the back seat and saw that Mickey Duck was holding three twenty-pound notes.

'Here, one for each of you and one for your other mate.'

'We don't want anything!' Bobby said, affronted.

'Speak for yourself,' I said, with fake delight, and

plucked the three twenties from Mickey Duck's fingers. Then I threaded my hand through Bobby's arm and pulled him away, his feet reluctantly following me up the street and back into Canberra Avenue.

'Don't look back,' I said. 'Let's see if Jack's in. Come on, we don't want them to think of us as anything except grateful kids.'

'But Tommy Young's garage!'

'Come on,' I said, fiercely.

We knocked for a few moments and watched as the red BMW turned out of the side street and went off in the opposite direction. Bobby seemed to deflate, exhaling all his breath in one go. Then the door opened and Jack was there, fully dressed, a football magazine under his arm.

'Where were you?' asked Bobby, walking straight past him into his house. I followed.

'Do come in,' said Jack. He turned and looked at me quizzically. 'What's wrong with your hair?'

I put my hand up to my head and remembered that I'd rushed out of the house. I knew I must have looked a sight.

'Never mind that,' I said, patting it down with the flat of my hand. 'Guess who we've just been talking to.'

'Mickey Duck, that's who,' said Bobby, before Jack could open his mouth. 'He had the Nike bag in the back of his car.'

Jack didn't look surprised.

We followed him into his kitchen. I noticed then that he had a new football shirt on which I hadn't seen before. It was that time of year when his dad kitted him out in the latest team strip. He sat down at the kitchen table. In front of him was a small pack of ten cigarettes sitting beside a mug of tea, the steam lazily leaking out of the top. I sat beside him.

'I thought you were going to get rid of it,' I said.

'I did get rid of it,' he replied. 'I put it in Tommy Young's lock-up.'

Neither of us answered. We just looked at him. He picked up his mug of tea and took a gulp from it.

'But Mickey Duck set the lock-up on fire,' said Bobby.

Jack shrugged.

'Someone could have got hurt.'

Jack shook his head. 'Nobody got hurt. I know that. I've been there.'

'We didn't see you!' I said.

'Earlier, much earlier. Before the fire engines.'

'How did Mickey Duck know the bag was there?' Bobby said.

'Someone must have told him.'

Jack was sitting, perfectly composed, holding his mug of tea with one hand and fiddling with the pack of cigarettes with the other. And yet there was something odd about him, something I couldn't put my finger on.

'But how did you get into Tommy's lock-up?' I said.

'Some kid I know from football. He's got keys'll fit anything.'

'And you did all this last night?' I said, perplexed.

He nodded. How typical. How absolutely classic. I'd been at my gran's and Bobby had been too upset by Tommy Young's attack to come out. I'd been away from the street, thinking about our future and worrying about whether a ladder had been left in or out of a cupboard, and without telling either of us, Jack had made plans, seen a friend, broken into a garage and caused a fire.

'I don't know why you two are looking so upset. This bloke attacked us yesterday, or have you forgotten? All I did was place the bag in his lock-up and make a quick, anonymous call to Mickey Duck.'

'But he never took the money,' Bobby said, weakly.

'It was YOU who mentioned his name to Mickey Duck. Not me. Not Jaz. YOU did it. That's why he came round here last night showing us up in the middle of the street!'

Jack was angry then, his mouth pulled across his teeth, his hands stiff, his fingers holding the cigarette packet and banging it on the table. I wanted to reach out and touch him. Actually I wanted to wrap my arms around him and feel my mouth on his skin. But Bobby was there and I couldn't.

'Maybe it's for the best,' I said, quietly, wishing this row was over and Bobby would go.

'Someone could have got hurt,' Bobby said, his voice in a whine.

'They didn't. And now Mickey Duck is sure that Tommy Young took the money. We are completely off the hook. Let them fight between themselves. They're all crooks. You know what the saying is. There's no honour among thieves!'

'Jack's right,' I said.

'He came after us last night and didn't care who was watching or what he did. He deserved what he got. I don't feel bad about it,' Jack continued, his voice softer.

'And don't forget about this,' I said, placing the three twenty-pound notes on the table.

'Pieces of silver,' Bobby said, unhappily. 'I don't want it.'

He turned and walked out of the room. As his footsteps sounded up the hall I heard him mumble, 'I'll see you two later.'

The front door shut and I sat looking at Jack.

'This is just between the two of us.'

I pushed the notes towards him but he waved them away. I pulled them back and put them into my pocket and looked at him. His new football shirt was vivid against his pale skin. I reached my hand out to touch his arm. He stayed still, hardly breathing, his head shaking from side to side. His skin was cold and I rubbed my fingers up and down, my chest and legs tingling at the touch.

'Tommy Young showed me up, Jaz, I had to do something.'

'I know,' I said, my mouth close to his ear.

I was hardly listening and just about to kiss him when he straightened up, his arms stiffening. I moved back a bit as he picked up the pack of ten and pulled off the cellophane. The cigarette pack lay open in front of him but he didn't take one. Just then I heard footsteps on the stairs and a moment later the kitchen door opened and his mum came in.

'Hi Jaz,' she said, and then, without taking breath, carried on talking to Jack: 'Remember, we're going shopping today, for college clothes. So don't be making any other arrangements.'

'I know.'

Jack pushed the cigarette packet away to the far end of the table and gave me a look of forbearance. His mum bustled out again, humming to herself.

'You could do with a haircut!' he said, his voice full of forced cheerfulness.

'You're right!' I stood up. 'I'll go home, get myself showered and have a complete makeover. Maybe I'll see you tonight?'

He shook his head. 'Football. I'll catch you tomorrow?'

'Yeah, sure. I'm a bit busy myself,' I lied, trying to hide my disappointment.

I leant over and kissed him lightly on the lips. When I left him he was fiddling with the neck of his new football shirt and didn't look up. I walked out of his house wondering what on earth I was going to do for the rest of the day. I shoved my hand in my jeans pocket and pulled out the three twenty-pound notes. It cheered me up. Just a little.

9

Later, I spent a bit of time hanging round the precinct seeing if anyone knew what had happened to Tommy Young. It wasn't long before Trevor Wilkins turned up with one of his mates, Marty, a nervous, quiet kid who was always sucking on an asthma inhaler. Trevor was confident that Tommy Young had gone to Majorca, to work in a mate's bar. Marty shook his head and in a whispery voice said he'd heard that Tommy had driven his Mustang up to Scotland to stay with his brother for a while.

I left them arguing about it and walked off. The important thing was that Tommy Young seemed to have left. This gave more credibility to the story that he had taken the money. Good. I had no sympathy for the man who had roughed up my two mates.

I went home in a listless mood. My mum was watching afternoon television and looked round when I walked into the room.

'You look awful,' she said.

First Jack and now my mum. I was beginning to feel paranoid. I went upstairs and looked in the long mirror in the bathroom. My eyes swept up and down, taking in my old jeans and creased T-shirt. Although

I'd combed my hair since the early morning it was still sticking out more one side than the other and looked shaggy. My face peeped out from below it, looking tired and pasty.

How had I let myself get so thoroughly *grubby*-looking? I wasn't unclean, I showered every day, but there was an uncared-for look about me, as though I couldn't be bothered. Was that the truth? That I couldn't care less about the way I looked?

Jack hadn't bothered much about appearances when we'd all been just friends, neither had he minded my casual dress and lack of make-up when we'd first got together. Lately, though, I'd noticed him taking a lot more care, always smelling strongly of aftershave, his hair often damp from being washed, and once or twice I'd gone into his house and found him ironing his shirts, placing them on hangers, the top buttons fastened to stop them creasing in the wardrobe.

I made a decision. I went to my wardrobe and had a tidy up. I dumped a lot of my clothes on the bed and had a sort through. Some things I put on hangers, some in the washing basket and a load got shoved in a black plastic bag for the charity shop. While I was doing it my mum popped her head into the room; she said she was going to see my gran and asked me if I wanted to come. I noticed she was carrying the embroidery and the watch that I'd picked up the night before.

'I'm a bit busy but give Gran my love,' I said. 'I'll go and see her at the weekend.'

'It's four weeks since you've been,' she said.

'At the weekend, definitely,' I said, irritably.

She gave me a long-suffering look and left. I felt instantly miffed. I had every intention of visiting Gran at the weekend. I lay on the floor and pulled out some old pairs of shoes from under the bed and put them into the black bag. Then I used a wire tie and fastened the bag as tightly as I could. My mum had a cheek. I did loads of things for Gran. Of course I was going to go and see her.

I struggled downstairs with the black bag and left it by the front door. Then I got my washing basket and put my clothes in the machine. After a few moments, watching it revolve, I put my hand in my pocket and pulled out the sixty quid that Mickey Duck had given me. It would pay for a decent haircut and some clothes. I might even have enough money left over to buy Gran a small box of Belgian chocolates. I perked up at this and rang the hairdresser's. The first appointment I could get was for the next morning.

I spent the evening in the bath, lying there and topping up the hot water until the skin on my fingers was dry and puckered, my face red, my hair damp with the steam. After drying myself I went downstairs and sat in my mum's chair, wrapped in a towelling dressing gown, and used the emery board on my nails. I felt scrubbed and squeaky clean and had an early night, drifting off to sleep to the sound of one of my CDs.

The hairdresser's was called Snips and as I walked into the shop the first person I saw was Penny Porter.

'Hi, Jaz,' she said, giving me a cheesy smile, showing dozens of teeth all at once.

I hadn't spoken to Penny Porter for years. She was in the year below us and lived away from the estate. I waited for my appointment and watched her moving round the shop, picking up towels, sweeping up hair, bringing cups of tea out to customers. Trust her to have a job there. It made me feel disgruntled. Possibly the fact that she had once been Jack's girlfriend (even though it was years before) made me feel awkward around her.

On top of that she just looked great. The stringy blonde hair had filled out and was hanging in a sheet on her shoulders. She was tall and thin but had breasts that stuck out considerably. I sat back, squaring my shoulders, and tried to make my breasts stick out further. The receptionist gave me an odd look and I relaxed back against the chair.

While I was having my hair cut Penny Porter brought me a cup of tea.

'How's Jack?' she asked, holding her head on one side.

'Good,' I answered. 'Busy, you know, pretty busy.'

'Right,' she said, tidying up a tray of perm curlers.

'Who's this *Jack*, Pen?' the stylist said. 'One of your boyfriends?'

I frowned and waited to see what Penny would say. She didn't speak, though; she just had this secret smile on her face and her shoulders seemed to twitch.

'Give him my regards, if you see him,' Penny said and walked off in a dazed way.

If I see him. Of course I was going to see him, but I wasn't going to mention Penny Porter. That was the trouble with having a secret boyfriend. It had its exciting moments but it also meant that I couldn't show him off, I couldn't claim him as mine. If Penny Porter had known that Jack and I were together she wouldn't have come over all dewy-eyed in front of me. I dismissed her from my mind and avoided looking at her for the rest of the time I was there.

My hair looked nice, I had to admit. The new shape suited my face. I had a blow dry as well, so it looked as though I had twice as much hair as before. I smiled at myself in the mirror. It was a good start and I walked out of the shop with my head high and caught myself looking in shop windows at my reflection.

I got a bus to the shopping centre. I walked round looking at things in shop windows and started to visualize myself going in to buy them. A hi-fi, a flat-screen telly, a holiday in Greece. In a few months I would be able to do just that. It gave me a good feeling for a few moments, but as that evaporated I began to feel uncomfortable. Tommy Young and his lock-up came into my head and I pictured the blackened door that was curling at the edges. Something unpleasant occurred to me. Tommy Young hadn't been in the lock-up but what if some kid had been in there, playing? Or nosing about? Just as we'd been doing almost a fortnight before when we found the money?

I pulled away from window shopping and made myself focus on finding some new jeans and a T-shirt. Afterwards I still had a few quid left out of the sixty pounds so I went into a chemist and looked at the make-up displays. I picked up a lipstick and put it smartly back when I saw that it was blood red. Another, further along the display, was a light plum colour, not unlike the natural colour of lips. I tried it on the back of my hand and it didn't look garish beside my pale skin.

I bought it and was walking away from the shop when I remembered Gran's Belgian chocolates. I tutted and pulled out all the change I had left. Hardly more than a couple of quid. At a corner shop, near home, I bought her a small bag of toffees.

At home I changed into the jeans and T-shirt and put on the lipstick. I went into my mum's room and sprayed on some of her perfume. I was bursting with anticipation as I walked along the road to Jack's house. What would he say? Would he like my hair? Would he be pleased that I was making more of an effort with my appearance?

Just as I came to his house his front door opened and he emerged with Bobby. They were both carrying fishing equipment. My heart sank.

'Hi!' Jack said, beaming with a smile, holding out a fishing rod. 'Guess where we're going.'

'Fishing?' I said, my voice coming from the bottom of my shoes.

Bobby was looking sheepish. The last time I'd seen him he'd gone off in a huff back to his own house. Now he and Jack were buddies again. I let my teeth grind against each other. Jack stood the fishing rod up against the wall and put his holdall down on the ground. He looked at me quizzically for a minute and my spirits lifted, I combed my fingers through the front of my new hairstyle and stood up straight, hoping he'd see the lipstick and the new clothes. He left Bobby fiddling with a bag and stepped across to me and spoke quietly in my ear.

'I'm taking Bobby fishing. To get his mind off Mickey Duck.'

He hadn't noticed a thing. I hardly registered what he said and I left a long gap for him to drop a compliment about the way I looked, but there was nothing.

'Can we have our money?' he said.

Money? For one bizarre moment I thought he meant *the* money. The suitcase of money. Then the penny dropped. He meant the money that Mickey Duck had given us the day before.

'I haven't got it,' I said.

'What do you mean?'

'I spent it.'

I said it defiantly and by that time Bobby was level with me and Jack and was listening.

'It wasn't yours to spend,' Jack said in a loud whisper.

'You said you didn't want it!'

'Not then. Not yesterday. We didn't want it yesterday because we were all . . . upset. We didn't mean we didn't want it at all.'

'Well, you should have made that clear,' I said, my voice a little high.

I stood rigidly in front of them. I could taste the lipstick on my mouth, greasy and sweet on my tongue. I smoothed down the unnoticed T-shirt and flicked my head so that my newly styled hair kept out of my eyes. They were both stumped. Bobby took Jack's arm.

'It doesn't matter. I never wanted that money anyway.'

'It does matter,' Jack said. 'It was for the three of us.'

I raised my voice then. It hadn't been a good couple of days and some simmering anger bubbled up in me.

'If you wanted the money,' I said, enunciating each word slowly. 'You should have said.'

'Come on,' said Bobby, pulling Jack's arm, 'let's go fishing.'

Jack gave me a last reproachful look and turned and walked off. I tried to swallow a lump of frustration and shoved my hands into the pockets of my new jeans. In one of them I found a twenty-pence piece. In the other was the lipstick. I pulled it out and looked at it for a moment. Then I chucked it across the road and walked off.

10

There was a police car parked in my gran's street and I faltered in my steps when I noticed it. It was a few doors on from her house and one of the officers was talking to a woman who was leaning on a nearby garden gate. The other was sitting in the car. Neither of them looked at me or in the direction of my gran's house so I tutted at my own jumpiness and opened the front door. Once inside I went straight upstairs to the landing and sat on the floor next to the banister. I didn't feel like going into any of my gran's rooms. I didn't feel much like doing anything. My friends had gone fishing. There was no one at home and nothing to do in the day that yawned ahead of me. I didn't even have a secret meeting planned with Jack to look forward to. More likely there would be frosty silence between us for a while.

I hadn't really intended to visit my gran's house again but I'd been swept there on a wave of annoyance. Where else could I go? I stretched my arms until my bones cracked and avoided the obvious answer: to the nursing home to see my gran. I could have taken the packet of toffees and got the bus that stopped right outside the building. Any of the care workers would have recognized me and waved me into the day room. We could have had some tea or sat out in the gardens. My gran would have been delighted to see me, I knew, calling me 'Janice, sweetheart.'

When she'd first gone into the home I'd visited her regularly. Once a week or so I'd turned up with some magazines or books and spent a couple of hours with her. She was still really bright then, cursing away at her frailty, her steely voice assuring me that she'd soon be home. We'd lounge in the warm sitting-room and I'd tell her any news there was about the family or her house or Mrs Reynolds, her neighbour. Then we'd talk about *Eastenders* or other soaps that she liked to watch on telly, discussing the characters or the story lines. After a few months, however, she seemed to lose some of her determination. I'd arrive and she wasn't dressed or she was dressed but her buttons were done up wrongly and she'd have one shoe and one slipper on. Sometimes her hair wasn't combed and her clothes were grubby and she didn't seem to notice. She started to repeat herself, telling me things that she'd told me the previous visit or mixing up characters in television programmes. She started to talk about her life in her own house as if she'd only been away from it a week or so. It was as if time had stopped for her. One weekend I couldn't go because I was ill and I felt this overwhelming sense of relief as the front door clicked and my mum and dad went instead.

My visits had lessened but I still cared for my gran.

I kept her house safe. I picked up anything that she needed. When I did go to see her I made myself stay for fifteen minutes longer than I'd planned. When I left I always gave her a hug, kissing her powdered cheek, and promised to come back soon. Had it really been four whole weeks since I had seen her?

I kicked my heel into the carpet. I'd had a lot on my mind.

Now I'd fallen out with my boyfriend over Mickey Duck's money and I was feeling guilty about it. It was easy for Jack. His parents were always slipping him cash and buying him things. I remembered his new football shirt and kicked my other heel into the carpet as well.

I looked upwards at the ceiling and the loft hatch and thought about the suitcase. All the money we wanted; in small notes, in bundles. Would it hurt for each of us to take one bundle out to spend? No one would have known. Why had Jack been so rigid?

I stood up, feeling restless, shaking my legs and arms. I needed to do something. The step ladder was leaning against the wall under the picture with the two kittens. A couple of days before I had been convinced that someone had moved it. I hadn't changed my mind, I'd just pushed the thought out of my head.

I pulled the ladder out, placing it under the loft hatch. Then I climbed up to the top step and, balancing carefully, reached up with both hands and pushed the hatch upwards. When it came loose I manoeuvred it slightly to the right, then let go and left it resting at an angle. I felt a blast of warm air coming from the loft and lowered my arms to give them a rest. After a few moments I reached up again and pushed the loft hatch away to the side. I wasn't tall enough or strong enough to hoist myself into the loft so I had to stand on tiptoes and stretch so that I could see.

It was hot, like a greenhouse, the sun's rays lying heavily on the tiled roof. It was dark except for little pinpoints of light that came through the tiles. The suitcase was to my left. I put out my hand and felt for it, grasping around in the shadowy light, trying to get at the handle. I pulled it along, noticing something at its side, dragging along beneath it. I edged the case towards me and carefully lowered it out of the loft hatch, stepping gingerly back down the ladder until I was at the bottom. I let it go and noticed my hands, filthy with the dust from the loft. I climbed up the steps again and felt around to see what had been stuck under the case. I pulled a piece of card towards me. As soon as I had it in my hand I realized it was a photograph. Puzzled, I came back down the ladder.

The photo was dirty where it had been on the floor of the loft, partly underneath the suitcase. I used the side of my hand to wipe off the dust. I frowned at the picture and looked down at the case. How could it have come out? The case was closed tightly. It had been securely fastened on the day Jack had put it up there. I had watched him.

Had someone been up in the loft and opened it?

I knelt down and unfastened the suitcase. The lid sprung up and there was the layer of photos. I shoved them to one side and found the money underneath, staring back at me, bundle after bundle, lying dormant, looking exactly as it had on the day we left it there.

What if there was one bundle missing? Or, perhaps, a couple of notes missing from each bundle? How would I know? I couldn't count it all again. Could I? I sat back, perplexed. Was I absolutely sure that photo had been in the case? It could have been up in the loft from some previous time. Perhaps it had been with other stuff of my gran's, left behind when the rest was shifted down when she went into the nursing home. I shook my head. My gran had told me that she never used the loft for anything. She said she couldn't be bothered to get someone to go all the way up there when she had plenty of room in the house for all her things. The only way that the photograph could have got into the loft was from the suitcase. Which meant that someone had been up there and opened it.

Apart from my mum and dad only myself and Jack had a key.

I couldn't relax. I kept walking to and fro along the landing, looking at the loft hatch and then back at the case.

Could Jack have gone up into the loft, opened the

case and taken some of the money? Why, though? He had been adamant that it should go up there in the first place. If he wanted money he only had to say and he could take it. I wouldn't argue.

What about Bobby?

He had no key. Short of breaking and entering how could he have got inside my gran's? Anyway Bobby was my friend, he had been for a long time. He hadn't even wanted to take the money. He'd only gone along with it to please me and Jack. I stared at the case for a few moments. There was only one sure way to find out: count the money. I knew how much it should be. Thirty thousand and six hundred pounds, give or take a few quid.

It would take for ever, though, and if I did count it that would mean I didn't trust one of my two closest friends. How could the three of us manage the next five and a half months if there was no trust? I looked again at the photograph and saw the faces of unfamiliar people in old-fashioned clothes. Could it have belonged to the previous occupants of the house? Left behind when they moved? I didn't know. I put it back into the case, moving the other photos so that they covered the money again. I had to push it out of my mind because there was no sure answer. I struggled up the ladder and with difficulty lifted the suitcase into the loft, pushing it as far away from the hatch as I could manage. When I got down again I stood for a moment, catching my breath. Being in the house, that close to the money, had provoked unwelcome thoughts. Most probably complete rubbish, brewing up in my head because I was angry at Jack and Bobby and because I felt a twinge of guilt about spending the sixty quid myself. I folded up the step ladder and put it back in the cupboard.

I decided to leave, going into the bathroom first to wash the dust off my hands and arms. While the tap was running I looked into the mirror and noticed my new hairstyle and T-shirt. I'd been so preoccupied I'd completely forgotten about my transformation. Maybe that's why Jack hadn't noticed it. He'd been mulling over the trouble with Tommy Young and at the same time trying to pacify Bobby. I was being too hard on him. So what if they wanted to go fishing? The more normal everybody looked the better.

I closed my gran's front door, taking care to lock the Chubb. I was jingling the key-ring in my hands as I walked down the road. I felt hungry all of a sudden and remembered the baker's round the corner where Bobby had bought doughnuts. That had been the day we'd first brought the money to my gran's. He'd taken my keys, I remembered. In spite of my revived mood the memory gave me an odd feeling. I turned the corner and headed for Freshbake.

I felt around in my pocket for what money I had left and was about to cross the road when my eye wandered along the row of shops. I knew them all from the years that I'd been visiting Gran: an off-licence, a bookie's and a chemist. The fifth shop along was a shoe repairer's. Across the window was fixed a neon light in lurid pink. It was new, I thought, or I certainly hadn't noticed it before. 'Keys Cut While U Wait', it said.

My appetite vanished.

Bobby had been gone a long time that morning, saying that he'd had to wait in the queue at the baker's. Jack and I had been messing around in the kitchen, too preoccupied with ourselves to worry about it. He'd had my gran's keys with him. Had he gone into that shop and had another set cut? Would he deceive us like that?

Why not? I thought, remembering the misplaced ladder and the stray photograph. Jack and I were deceiving him, after all.

11

It was gone eleven that night when Jack knocked on my front door. I was still up but my mum and dad had gone to bed. Jack had his fishing stuff hanging over one arm and he looked exhausted.

'Come to my house for a while,' he said. 'My mum and dad are out.'

'I can't, I'm tired,' I said, huffily.

'Go on,' he whispered, stepping nearer to me.

His face was close to mine and I could feel his hair on my cheek. He smelled of grass and earth and I could almost feel the heat from the day coming off his clothes.

'Just for a while,' I said, stupidly.

'By the way,' he said, walking down my path, 'I like the hair!'

I smiled in spite of myself. The annoyance I had felt during the day was suddenly swept aside because I was pleased to see him. All the bad thoughts I'd had were forgotten with the prospect of being with him (I had no pride, that had always been my trouble).

Half an hour later I was in his room, the lights low and the music on in the background. My new T-shirt was lying by the pillow, a crumpled mess, my new hairstyle sticking up, my neck wet with perspiration. He was half sitting, half lying, playing with his unopened pack of ten cigarettes. I had my arms across my chest covering myself, my bra hanging off one shoulder.

He smelled of soap now and his hair was wet from the shower. He hadn't bothered to get dressed again and was wearing paisley-patterned boxer shorts. Every now and again his fingers reached for the zip of my jeans, but that was where it stopped. Like a padlock, the zip stayed fastened and that was how I wanted it.

'You can't blame me for trying,' he whispered, his voice hoarse.

'I can,' I said.

I sat up, pulling my clothes back together, lifting my feet off the bed. It was gone twelve and I knew I should go home before his parents came back. In the beginning, we had only wanted to keep our secret from Bobby, but that had meant keeping everyone else in the dark as well. Now it was natural for us to take care.

'I'm sorry about the money,' I said, for the tenth time, pulling my T-shirt roughly over my hair, destroying any remains of a tidy hairstyle.

'Forget it,' said Jack, tossing the pack of cigarettes into the air and catching them again. 'We were all a bit stressed. Now that Tommy Young and Mickey are off our backs we should all begin to relax.'

It was on the tip of my tongue to say something about my worries of the morning, the ladder, the photograph and the keys. But since Jack had called my mood had softened and my suspicions had wavered. He was still talking, his voice quiet and serious, so I leant back against his headboard and listened.

'We've got to trust each other. We can't afford to fall out over anything. That's why I spent the day with Bob. The last thing I felt like doing was fishing. But he needed a lot of reassurance. You know how uncertain he was at the beginning. If he decides that he doesn't want to go on with it we'll all lose out.'

I nodded. He was right. Bobby had been the nervous one. The idea that he would go and have a second key cut was ridiculous. He wouldn't have the nerve and anyway he was just too honest.

'We've got to keep cool. The worst of it is over now that Mickey Duck thinks Tommy Young took the money. All we have to do is wait.'

I went home feeling better than I had all day. My mum and dad were already asleep and I locked the front door, got myself some water and went to bed. Before I dozed off I let myself think of Jack and me, lying together, less than half an hour before, his skin against mine, his hair tickling my face. The memory made my chest ache and I pushed myself into the pillow, winding the duvet around my legs. Me and Jack and Bobby; the money in the suitcase; it was all going to be all right, I was sure.

But the next morning everything changed.

I got a phone call from Jack about eleven. I was dressed but I hadn't planned to go out and see either him or Bobby today. My mum had insisted on some time at home, clearing up my bedroom, helping with the house chores. When she handed me the phone she gave me a warning look, as if to say, *You're not going out!* I hardly had time to say hello before Jack spoke.

'Come to Bobby's as soon as you can. It's important.'

'I can't!' I said, eyeing my mum's back disappearing moodily into the kitchen.

'As soon as you can. Just come as soon as you can get away.'

Then the phone went dead and I stood wondering what he wanted, what the rush was for. Jack's tone had been serious and it was something to do with Bobby, not me and him. That meant it concerned the money.

I could hear my mum clattering plates around from the kitchen so I picked up the pen and wrote quickly on the message pad.

Just popped out. Be back in half an hour. Honest. Love Janice.

Bobby opened the door straight away. He looked as though he'd seen a ghost.

'What's the matter?' I asked.

'In here.'

He led me into the back dining-room, a place we hardly ever went. Jack was there, standing, half leaning against a giant wooden dining-table. I was puzzled and looked from one to the other. The room was enveloped in shadows, just a splash of light from a small, heavily draped window. Brown furniture was everywhere, the chairs locked into the table, rigid and uninviting. The house was silent. I guessed his mum was out at work.

'What's up?' I said, apprehensively.

'You tell her,' Bobby said, his mouth in a sulky line.

'Bobby's had a visitor. Billy Ross. He came round about an hour ago.'

'Billy Ross?' I said, picturing the man with the huge stomach and gold teeth.

'He knows about the money,' Bobby interrupted, his voice shaky.

'How could he?' I said, with a half-laugh. 'We just saw him and Mickey Duck the other day. They found the bag in Tommy Young's lock-up. You were there. Mickey Duck was so pleased he gave us money.'

I stuttered a little at the 'money', seeing as I'd spent it on myself.

'He came round here an hour ago. He threatened me. He knows we've got the money!'

Bobby was clenching his fists, his head bent forward.

'I don't get it,' I said, confused.

'He brought this.'

Jack pushed something towards me. It had been lying on the table and I hadn't noticed. A small piece of plastic, one side of it jagged as though it had been cut with scissors. I picked it up, my fingers brushing the polished surface of the wood.

'What is it?' I said, needlessly, turning it over. It was half of a cash card. I could just see the beginnings of Bobby's signature.

'I lost it. You remember. I was looking for it for days.'

'And Billy Ross gave it to you?' I said.

'He says he found it on Mickey Duck's living-room floor.'

'You had it on you that night?'

I looked at him with surprise. It was the first I'd heard of it.

'I'm not sure. I didn't think so, at the time. I had my black jeans on and maybe I had the card in my back pocket,' said Bobby. 'I'm just not sure.'

'You didn't notice it was gone?'

Bobby, who was always checking his money and his bus pass, hadn't *noticed* that he'd lost his cash card?

'I did. The next day, maybe a couple of days later. Thing is, once we took that money and hid it I had other things on my mind.'

There was tension in the room. It sat between us, as solidly as the old furniture. I looked down at the wooden table and traced my finger along the edge.

'Why didn't he show it to Mickey Duck?' I said.

'He wants it for himself.'

'The money?'

'Not all of it. Just ten thousand. For ten thousand he said he'll give me the other half of my card.'

I was speechless. A whole story unfolded in my head.

The big man, his gold teeth glinting under Mickey Duck's bare lightbulb, bending down and just happening to find Bobby's cash card on the living-room floor. I imagined him tucking it away in his pocket, making plans for later. He wanted ten thousand pounds. Why not all of it? It didn't sit right.

'What are we going to do?' said Jack.

'Pay him!' said Bobby. 'Pay him. It's only ten thousand.'

Only ten thousand. Bobby was talking as if it was a game of Monopoly. *Pass Go Collect Two Hundred Pounds.* My eyes swept over him. He had a white T-shirt on, tucked into some jogging trousers. The T-shirt had been ironed to perfection, a thin crease down each sleeve. I imagined him, leaning over the ironing board, spraying steam on to the shirt, his clean jogging trousers hanging over the back of a chair, smelling of soap and fresh air. A knock at the door breaking through the quiet of his house. On the doorstep a big man with two gold teeth and half a cash card. The whole thing irritated me.

'But why should we pay him? So he's got Bobby's card. He could have found it anywhere. On the pavement, on the road, anywhere. He could be bluffing, trying to trick us.'

Jack looked at me, puzzled.

'What's the likelihood of that? Billy Ross just happens upon Bobby's cash card lying on the street and makes up a cunning plan.'

'But he's Mickey Duck's mate!' I said.

'Ten thousand pounds is a lot of money. Maybe he's not that much of a mate.'

I didn't know what to say. It was the last thing we had expected. Why now? Why not two weeks ago when the money first went missing?

'Did he say where and when he wants this money?' I demanded.

'Friday night. At the boathouse at nine o'clock.'

'I can't talk about this now,' I said, wanting to be alone. 'I'll meet you later but not here.'

'Where?'

'At yours, Jack. About four, this afternoon. Then we can decide what to do.'

Bobby put his hand on my arm. I could feel a slight tremble in his fingers. His eyes looked puffy, as if he'd been crying. I wanted to feel sorry for him, I knew how upset he'd been when Tommy Young had attacked him. But all I could feel was anger. How could he have dropped his card in that living-room? How could he?

'I'm going,' I said, gently shaking off his arm.

They both nodded and I left them and walked back to my own house. Halfway there I stopped and looked round. I half expected to see someone hanging around, watching me. The street was empty, though. When I opened my front door my mum was there, looking thoroughly fed up.

'Don't say a word,' I said, firmly but lightly, and went up to my room to start tidying up.

12

I don't know exactly when the idea first came to me. It was when I was tidying up my room, some time between stripping my bed and vacuuming under it. My mum came in and looked at me with surprise. I wasn't much of a cleaner, in fact it was a job that I hated. Still, today, I found myself working at a feverish pace, emptying my shelves of old books and magazines, and cleaning underneath; tidying my drawers out, throwing away half-empty tubes of cream and bits of old make-up; folding up my underwear and coupling my socks.

All the while I was doing this my mind seemed to be on hold. It was there, the idea, but it was sort of frozen, as if the words had been printed on to paper and left for me to look at from time to time.

Bobby made the whole story up.

I dusted the surfaces and used a spray glass-cleaner to wipe the mirror and the windows. I tidied stuff back into my drawers and then, when there was nothing more I could do, I flopped down on the bed and looked at my thoughts again.

Bobby made the whole story up.

It was an outrageous thing to think and yet

somehow, between the washing and tidying, it had popped into my head and refused to go away. I could have dismissed it immediately. I didn't, though, I let it sit there and it became more solid by the minute.

Bobby said that he had lost his cash card on that Saturday night, even though he hadn't mentioned it at the time. How likely was that? Bobby was the most careful of the three of us. He knew what he had in either of his two bank accounts to the nearest penny. My financial affairs were completely haphazard, my first cash card eaten up by the machine months before. The second one lost along with my mobile phone. I was hopeless at taking care of things. Jack didn't even have an account and was always searching his pockets and drawers to find the odd fiver that he'd tucked away earlier.

It was a week and a half since we'd taken the money. Bobby had been reluctant at first, scandalized by the very thought of it. After meeting Mickey Duck he had worried away at it driving me and Jack nuts. Could it have all been an act? There was the step ladder in my gran's house which had most definitely been moved. Then the photograph. Someone had been at the suitcase. It wasn't Jack, I was sure, and it hadn't been me. Who else could it have been except Bobby?

He could have had a key cut. Decided, right from the very beginning, that he wasn't going to work with us. That he was going to have more than his share of the money. But this was *Bobby* I was thinking about!

One of my best friends, someone I should have trusted with my deepest secrets. The three of us were mates. Why would Bobby turn against us like that? Why would he?

And then something occurred to me.

Could he have found out about me and Jack? Had he seen us kissing? Was he annoyed with us, hurt that we had kept it a secret? Had he found out in those weeks before we discovered the money, when Jack and I were fooling around behind his back; almost, at times, under his nose? When we were enjoying the secrecy, feeding off it recklessly for some sort of excitement? Had he seen us in his bedroom, or in Jack's kitchen? Or in my living-room? There were times, during those weeks, when he had been fed up and seemed depressed. I had put it down to worry over the exams but maybe he had found out that Jack and I were more than friends. While we thought we had a secret, had he felt left out, lied to, betrayed?

I stood up and paced the room, thinking hard. The obvious thing to do was to have it out with Bobby face to face. To tell him what I thought. That's what friends would do. But it meant admitting that Jack and I had lied to him about our relationship. And if I was completely wrong about the money and the cash card then Bobby and Jack would be furious with me. It would be as though I and not Bobby had betrayed our friendship, the silly oath we had taken on the night we took the money. I banged my fists together. I had no idea what to do.

If only I had counted the money. Then I could be sure.

I wanted to talk to Jack about it. He would know what to do. Most probably he would argue me out of it, show me how it was impossible. Then I would feel better about it.

But later that afternoon, when I arrived at his house, Bobby was already there. Judging by the empty Coke cans and fried chicken boxes he'd been there all day. I was immediately annoyed. Bobby had had the whole day to get round Jack. First there was the fishing expedition, now this. It seemed as though Jack was spending a lot more time with Bobby than with me. I sat in the corner, my legs tucked up tightly underneath me.

'We've been talking about it non-stop,' Jack said.

I nodded.

'We'll have to pay up. It's the only way to get Billy Ross off our backs. It's not the end of the world. We'll still have about seven thousand each.'

About seven thousand pounds each. It didn't sound so bad. Unless Bobby had made it all up, which meant that he would end up with seventeen thousand.

'I still think it might be a bluff,' I said, carefully.

'How?' Jack said.

'This Billy Ross, he doesn't know for sure that we've got the money. What if we just keep quiet, not turn up on Friday night. What can he do?'

'Tell Mickey Duck?' said Bobby.

'Then we'll just deny it. It's his word against ours. We could say that the cash card was dropped in the street behind his garden. We admitted to being there.'

'It's all right for you to say that. It's my cash card. One word and Mickey Duck'll be round here with a petrol rag through my letter box. How would you feel if that was hanging over your head?'

I didn't speak. He had a point.

'Bobby's right. It's too dangerous to chance it. That business with Tommy Young? I had no idea that he would torch his garage. I suppose, truthfully, I just didn't think. I was angry and just did it. This time, though, we have to be careful, to think it through.'

'If we give him the money, it'll get him off our backs.'

'What if he wants more?'

'He won't.' Bobby said it with certainty.

'How do you know?' I demanded.

'Because I won't give it to him unless he gives me my cash card back. Then he's got no hold on us.'

'*You* won't give it to him?' I said, irked by Bobby taking charge all of a sudden.

'Bobby wants to take the money. I said I'd go with him but he wants to go alone,' Jack chipped in.

'I'm the one who dropped the cash card so I've got most to lose out of this. I want to get it sorted myself,' said Bobby.

I sat back and looked at the two of them. Jack was nodding in agreement with Bobby. I was amazed that he couldn't see that something was wrong. This wasn't like Bobby at all. Bobby was the least brave of the three of us. In five years I don't think he ever bunked a day off school. 'What if my mum finds out?' was all he ever said.

'Jaz, you go to your gran's and pack the money up. Then me and you will wait at the yellow jetty. We'll only be a couple of hundred metres away from Bobby if he needs us.'

My mouth opened. Now Jack was including me in plans that had been made earlier, assuming that I would just go along with what they had decided.

'It's for the best. We'll still have over seven thousand each.'

The sound of Jack's ring tone interrupted us. He got up and went across to the chest of drawers and picked up his mobile. I could hear him saying *Hello? Oh hi* . . . I couldn't concentrate. I was so annoyed I could hardly swallow. I had been outvoted without having my say. Bobby seemed more relaxed and I glanced again at his white T-shirt, which even after a day's wear looked as though he had just put it on. Looking down I saw grey trainers that didn't have a mark on them – the soles looked like they could bounce around the room. Brand new, expensive-looking; probably not much change from a hundred pounds.

'They're nice,' I said, coughing to clear my throat.

He looked down.

'My uncle gave me some money. Remember, I told you?'

His uncle at the other end of the tube line. How convenient.

Jack was saying goodbye. *Nice to hear from you. Yes, I'll see you around.* He came across and sat down again, a funny expression on his face.

'That was Penny Porter,' he said.

'Right,' I said, not really registering the name.

'She just wanted a chat,' he said, mysteriously.

'I'd better go,' I said.

'But about the money, Jaz,' said Jack. 'Are you in agreement? Should we give the money over?'

'Why not,' I said, my voice light but my shoulders plaited up.

I left then. I went into my house and picked up my gran's keys. Taking care that neither Bobby nor Jack was following me, I walked straight through the park to her house. Once inside I went upstairs to the landing and with some difficulty got the case down out of the loft and opened it for the second time in a couple of days.

I got some paper and a pen from my gran's bedroom and laid the money out along the landing. Then I sat down cross-legged on the floor and began to count it, bundle by bundle, noting down the amount in each one. I did it slowly and carefully, using my forefinger, licking it from time to time and flicking the corners of the notes up one by one. Afterwards I placed the counted bundles back into the case so that there was no chance of me counting anything twice.

It took just over an hour. My piece of paper was covered in a list of amounts. I could add them up manually but I wasn't sure I was up to it. I decided to put the case away again and head for home. After a bit of a struggle I closed up the loft hatch and tucked the piece of paper into my back pocket. Then I went home. Once indoors I went up to my bedroom and fished out a calculator from my desk drawer.

I did the sum carefully, taking it slowly, adding up five numbers at a go and then carrying the total forward. I started at the top of the page and worked my way down. Then, to be absolutely sure, I did it from the bottom and worked upwards. I came to the same total both times.

Twenty-nine thousand and seventy pounds.

Over a thousand pounds was missing. I'd proved my point but I didn't feel good about it.

13

The old boathouse was up by the lake, very close to the area where Jack, Bobby and many others sat on their fishing stools, surrounded by boxes of maggots and sandwiches wrapped in tin foil. It was a single-storey wooden building and years ago it had been used to store rowing boats and canoes that people hired out in the summer months. It had been shut for the past two or three years. The paint was peeling and several of the small leaded windows had been smashed. The council had surrounded it with a flimsy wire fence and security notices. They wanted to knock it down but local residents argued that it should be made a listed building and restored. The end result was that it was a place that kids played in and around during the day. There was a long, winding tarmac lane that linked it with the road: it was a good route to the lake for those with bikes.

Bobby said that he had to give the money to Billy Ross at nine o'clock. That meant there shouldn't be many people around.

It was a fiercely hot day, the clouds covering the sun, the air thick, every footstep seeming like an effort. I'd noticed how empty the streets were when I went to my gran's in the late afternoon to pack the bag. In the park there were kids lying flat out on the grass, the swings hanging listlessly and the roundabout idling. The footballs sat still and the bikes were resting on their sides. Only the ice-cream man looked happy, giving out greasy-looking '99s and wiping his hands from time to time on a grubby tea cloth.

Towards the edge of the park I saw Penny Porter with another girl on a bench. She waved to me, her mouth breaking into a smile. She had sunglasses on even though there was no need. Her hair was clipped back off her face, making her look cool and composed. I put my fingers up and tried to pull my fringe down over my hot forehead, but it flicked back. I quickened my pace, sensing that she wanted me to stop and talk. I pointed at my watch and made signals to convey to her that I was in a rush.

The money was to go into an old rucksack that Jack had given to me. It was plain black with no logo or brand name on it. He had pointed out the zip and Velcro fastenings several times, as though I was a small child and had to be carefully instructed.

It took me quite a while and I agonized as I did it, gazing for a long time at the bundles of notes as they lay in my gran's old suitcase. It didn't seem right to disturb them but in the end I did. I packed the black bag carefully, the bundles sitting among some old bubble wrap I'd found. I walked back home, through the park, with it slung casually over one shoulder, not wanting to look as if I was carrying anything important.

As I went indoors I passed my mum who was just going out, holding the car keys and a couple of carrier bags.

'What's up?' I asked.

'I'm not sure. Gran needs to see me,' she said. 'I'll tell you about it later.'

I watched as the car drove off leaving a trail of hot exhaust behind it in the street. Then I went indoors and up to my bedroom. I lay flat on my bed, the black rucksack beside me, and thought about the evening ahead. I imagined Bobby walking along, the bag across his back, heading for the old boathouse while Jack and I sat on the jetty, our feet centimetres from the lake, waiting for him to make a cash delivery. And if I was right? If there was no Billy Ross? Would he hide the money somewhere in or around the boathouse and go back to retrieve it later? I chewed at my bottom lip.

I still hadn't told Jack. Most people wouldn't believe this. Why not? This was a niggling worry to me. There had been times, over the past couple of days, when I could have dropped into his house and seen him, got him on his own, explained it carefully to him.

I told myself I was afraid that he would laugh it off, tell me not to be silly. I thought he might even confront Bobby there and then. And if he did that how would we ever know for sure? Bobby might insist that he was telling the truth, might go with the money to the old boathouse and wait. When no one turned up he would just shrug his shoulders and say that Billy Ross had got cold feet. How could we prove otherwise? We could hardly walk up to the man and say, 'Did you try to blackmail our friend?'

But it wasn't just that. The truth was I felt physically divided off from the pair of them, as though there was this invisible wall between us. I couldn't have told Jack. Over the past couple of days he had been withdrawn. He'd spent masses of time with Bobby trying to 'calm him down', he said. When the three of us had been together he'd seemed to be sitting close to Bobby, listening to him, hardly including me in the conversation. True, I'd been distant with Bobby, perhaps even with Jack. I was annoyed that we were going along with this plan to give away a third of our money.

As the evening approached, though, I began to feel better. When Bobby went off to the boathouse I would tell Jack. Then afterwards Jack and I could go back and search for the bag. If we found it (and I was sure we would) then we would know that Bobby had tried to trick us.

We got there miles too early.

'I don't want to be late,' Bobby had said, tersely.

We were on the tarmac lane that led up to the old boathouse. Even though it was only eight-forty he was walking ahead, his steps purposeful, as though he really did have an appointment with someone. It was still light but the overhanging branches hid the sky and the lane itself was shadowy. Halfway up, Jack and I peeled off into the bushes.

'We're going to wait by the yellow jetty. We'll keep out of sight but if you want us to come just shout. We'll be able to hear you.'

Bobby nodded and we left him standing uncertainly in the lane. He looked like a little lost schoolboy and for a moment I faltered and wondered whether I was mad not to believe him. When I looked back a second or two later he had completely disappeared. I turned and followed Jack to the lake.

The yellow jetty wasn't really yellow. It was a landing place for boats and it had a stripe of colour along the edge, but that was flaking and dull and looked more like a dirty beige than yellow. We sat on the dry wood and leaned back against the wooden posts. In front of us the lake was absolutely still, the water dark and soupy with flotillas of lilies just undulating on the surface. In places there were clouds of midges but elsewhere it looked clear and across the water I could see a heron, standing to attention on a branch. Another day, another time I would have pointed it out to Jack. He wasn't interested, though. He'd pulled his mobile out of his pocket and was studying the screen. He looked thoughtful, his forehead stiff. I was building up to speak to him but he started talking first.

'I don't feel happy about this. Not happy at all. I don't think Bobby should be on his own . . .'

I had my mouth open to answer but stopped when Jack let his head drop into his hands.

'Maybe it would have been better if we'd left the money where it was.'

I was surprised to hear such a thing coming from him. He'd been the leader, the decisive one. He'd physically carried the money away from Mickey Duck's house, kept it in his room overnight, made plans for it, got us to swear an oath. It was disconcerting to hear him sound unsure. We had done the right thing. Of course we had. Anyone in our position would have taken that money.

'I thought it would be easy,' he said. 'Just forget about it for six months. Have a few quid to spend when we're at college. Simple.'

'But it is easy,' I said, all thoughts of Bobby slipping from my mind.

'We've got Mickey Duck watching us. Tommy Young with a grudge. Now we're being blackmailed.'

'But that's just the point,' I said. 'I don't think that Billy Ross really did—'

But I was interrupted by a rattle of leaves and the sound of wheels scrunching up the gravel. Two bikes appeared out of the bushes. On the one in front was Trevor Wilkins. This time he had no stories to tell. He was just being nosy.

'What you two up to?' he said in a sarcastic voice. His mate laughed.

'Past your bedtime, Wilkins,' said Jack.

'Got any cigarettes?' he asked, looking hopeful.

'Get lost, Trevor!' Jack's voice lowered to a hiss.

Trevor looked momentarily confused and then shrugged his shoulders.

'Suit yourself.'

He turned his bike back into the bushes and his mate followed. I watched for a moment until the forest swallowed them both up. When we were alone again I looked back to the lake and saw that the sky had darkened suddenly. In just seconds, it seemed, I could see less than before. I rubbed my eyes but the far shore had become just a mass of grey shapes and the water darker. Once the boys had gone everything seemed quieter; there was only Jack's voice, soft against the night.

'I blame myself. We should have left the money where it was . . .'

His shoulders were sloped and his chin was dipping into his chest. He was beginning to sound like Bobby. He'd been spending far too much time with him and it had shaken his confidence. I had to tell him what I thought.

'I don't think Bobby is being straight with us—'

I didn't get to finish, though. The sound of a car in the distance made us both look round. It came from the direction of the boathouse. Jack stiffened up and put his finger over his lips.

'It's probably the park ranger,' I whispered, looking at my watch.

It was five to nine and I wasn't expecting anyone anyway. A moment later we both heard a car door slam. It was quick and hard like the crack of a whip.

'It's him, I'll bet,' Jack said, pulling himself up to a standing position.

'No, look . . .'

There wasn't any time to tell him and he wasn't in the mood to listen. I had missed my moment. There was a deep silence and I could almost feel the darkness descending, wrapping itself around us. Jack's head was cocked and his face was closed tight against me. He was listening for every sound, hoping that words might carry across the distance. But there was nothing, not a squeak, and I shook my head. How could there be any sounds? Bobby wasn't meeting anyone. I had known it all along.

Jack started to walk along the jetty towards the bushes. I followed him but he held his hand up like a policeman at traffic lights, letting me know that I had to stop where I was. It exasperated me. I felt like stamping my feet with temper but I just stood simmering quietly. Why not wait, I thought. In a few minutes Bobby would appear through the bushes, a smile on his face, telling us that it was all over.

But it didn't happen like that.

Instead there was a shout. It sounded like the word 'NO!' but I couldn't be sure. Jack's face crumbled. Then we heard another sound. A scream.

Jack ran off into the blackness of the bushes and I

followed. He flew ahead of me, crashing through foliage and bending back branches so that they whiplashed and hit me as I struggled to keep up, watching my footing in the tangled undergrowth. As we got closer the words got louder.

'No! Stop. No, I don't know! I DON'T KNOW!'

With every word Jack seemed to leap ahead. He had been expecting something bad and he had been right. All the way behind him I felt this hollowness in my chest as though a great hole was opening up inside me.

'No, no, DON'T KNOW! I don't know . . .'

Jack got there a couple of seconds ahead of me. As I emerged from the bushes my face dropped in shock. There was a car parked at an angle, its door hanging open. Beside it, Billy Ross was standing, his face twisted in rage. He had Bobby by the throat, pinned up against the car. On the ground a few feet away was the black bag, the bundles tipped out on to the earth, one of them torn open, showing a couple of ten-pound notes and dozens of small note-sized sheets of newspaper.

'Stop!' Jack shouted. 'What are you doing? Just take the money!'

He pointed to the bag and the tipped out bundles. It was too dark for him to see what was there. I stood absolutely still, my feet rooted to the ground. Bobby was leaning backwards over the car; he was bleeding from his mouth or nose, I wasn't sure which. I thought he was crying as well, his shoulders rising and falling. Billy Ross had his hand at Bobby's throat, holding him tightly, his huge stomach like a boulder, weighing down on him.

The man swore out loud; one curse after another. 'There's no money in the bastard bag!' he shouted.

'I didn't know . . .' Bobby said.

At that moment Billy Ross's arm went back and then swung forward, his hand slapping Bobby's face hard, sending his words back down his throat so that he seemed to gargle quietly for a few seconds. He went limp against the car, like a rag doll, only staying up because Billy Ross was holding him there.

Jack ran towards the big man.

'Ring the police,' he said, throwing his mobile at me.

I caught it clumsily and noticed my hands shaking with fright. *Call the police!* How could I call them? How would it be explained? But there was no time to think because by that time Jack had jumped up on to Billy Ross's side and hooked his arms around the man's neck.

My fingers were trembling as I stabbed at the numbers on the tiny mobile.

'POLICE! POLICE!' I shouted, making my voice as loud as possible.

Jack had wrapped his legs around Billy Ross's stomach and was using his weight to try and pull him away from Bobby, who seemed to have passed out.

'There's no money! It's all fake!' Billy Ross screamed.

'POLICE!' I shouted to the operator. 'THE COOK ESTATE. COME TO THE BOATHOUSE AT HERON LAKE!'

'You kids should have kept out of it. You can't play around with people like me! This is not some game!'

Billy Ross grunted out the words while twisting back and forth until, with a heave, he finally threw Jack off his side and let go of Bobby. Jack stumbled backwards and fell on to the soft earth, and Bobby seemed to slide down the car until he was sitting on the ground, his hands covering his face. I could hear squeaking from the mobile and when I put it up to my ear the operator was asking me to explain.

'The old boathouse. At Heron lake. Near the Cook Estate. Quick! Someone's been hurt,' I answered, my words falling over each other.

Billy Ross walked over to the black bag and picked it up, pulling one of the bundles out. He threw it at Jack and then chucked the bag in the direction of Bobby. That's when he seemed to notice me and the mobile phone in my hand.

'Please hurry,' I said to the operator.

He snatched it from me and threw it into the bushes. Then he shoved me viciously in the shoulder and I tumbled back on to the tarmac.

'A bunch of kids! You won't make a bastard monkey out of me!'

He spat the words out and seemed to be walking towards me when in the distance, like a distressed bird, I heard the siren of a police car. Behind him, I could see Jack struggling to get to his feet and I heard his voice, shaky but loud.

'I'll tell Mickey Duck. I'll tell him everything about this. He'll know you tried to go behind his back.'

Billy Ross ignored him and took hold of Bobby's shoulder, flinging him away from the car. He got in and started it up, slamming the door hard. The siren was still some distance away as he reversed sharply and shunted forwards a couple of times, Bobby rolling himself out of the way of the wheels. When the car was facing in the opposite direction Billy leaned out of the window and pointed at the three of us.

'Just watch your backs! Keep looking over your shoulders. I'll be somewhere around.'

And the car shot off, as though it was at the start of a race. It turned into the lane and we could hear its wheels on the tarmac and the thrust of the engine as it accelerated away. It was over. That's what I honestly thought. I looked in dismay at the tipped-over bag and the bundles of notes that I had spent hours putting together. Cutting the newspapers up into the right size, using real ten-pound notes like bookends, packing it all up so that at first glance it looked like the real thing. Only it was supposed to be Bobby who discovered the truth, not Billy Ross.

Jack was helping Bobby to his feet when we heard

the screech of brakes and the bang. A cry hit the air and then the more distant sound of the car engine revving up and speeding away again. I walked towards the noise, Jack following me close behind. I could hear the sounds of shouting and panic. The lane was dark by then but round the bend I could see the shape of a boy straddling a bike, standing still and pointing at something.

I got up close. It was Marty, Trevor Wilkins' mate. I looked in the direction that he was pointing. There was a bike on the tarmac, lying on its side, its wheels buckled. I could hear Jack's voice behind me and from somewhere in front of me, down on the main road, the sound of the police siren.

I saw the shape on the ground about twenty metres away. It was like a sack lying in the middle of the lane, a heap of something. As I walked slowly towards it a terrible feeling took hold of me. With every step my feet became heavier and I knew without even having to look what had happened. The siren sounded irritated and as though it was only a short distance away, further down the lane.

Trevor Wilkins was lying on his back, his head turned to the side. His arms and legs were splayed out. From behind me I could hear Marty's voice.

'The car hit him. It went right over him.'

I knelt down beside him. There was blood on his face and he looked as though he was asleep. Trevor Wilkins, who was always full of information, who always had his nose into everyone else's business, was silent.

Jack was behind me.

'Oh God, what's happened here? Is he badly hurt?'

I just nodded my head. Anybody, any fool, could see that the boy was badly hurt.

14

Jack and I sat in Casualty in frosty silence. He was staring at his mobile, pressing buttons, shaking it, trying to see if it was still working. Bobby had needed stitches for a cut across his nose and above his eye and the nurse had taken him into the treatment area. Not that he'd said much to me. I was enemy number one.

The police had only asked a couple of questions and taken our names and addresses. *Was it us who had made the 999 call?* Yes. (We let them think that the call was made as a result of the accident and not moments before it.) *Did we see the car that ran over the boy?* Yes, but only from a distance. *Did we see the man driving it?* No, not clearly enough. *What were we doing there at that time of night?* Just hanging around. *Why was Bobby injured?* He and Jack had an argument that got out of hand.

Trevor Wilkins was in the operating theatre. We had no idea how he was. His mum, Chrissie, arrived when we'd been there for about thirty minutes. She was a small, thin woman with white blonde hair and a perpetual tan. She came running in wearing flip-flops, a tiny black handbag flying out behind her. I watched her go up to the desk and heard her voice, urgent, worried, but I didn't hear the words. A nurse appeared out of nowhere and took her by the elbow through Casualty and off down a corridor. I could hear the flip-flops slapping against the floor as she passed us.

Just looking at her made my chest tighten.

Some time later Bobby's mum appeared. The lift doors opened and Mrs Parsons burst out, still in her nurse's uniform, walking purposefully towards us, using her hands to roll up invisible sleeves. We both stood up, as though the head teacher had just walked into the room.

'What happened?' she said, looking from Jack to me and then back again.

'There was an argument. It got out of hand. It was hot, he was needling me. One thing led to another. He fell over, I fell over,' said Jack, holding out his bruised arm, his skin grazed and raw-looking. 'Bobby knocked his head on a rock. I thought it better to bring him here, just to check that he was all right.'

'For God's sake,' she said, 'I thought you were supposed to be friends!'

'We just had a row.' Jack shrugged his shoulders and I nodded in agreement. Jack sounded so sincere, the lie taking on a reality of its own.

She tutted, her eyes avoiding either of us. Then she walked off towards the reception desk. After being pointed in the right direction she disappeared behind the same door as Chrissie Wilkins.

On the floor beneath Jack's feet was the black rucksack containing the fake money. For a while, I had been unable to explain it. The shock of seeing Billy Ross and then the accident had left me literally speechless. What could I say? Bobby had looked at me with disgust, as though I was muck under his shoes. Jack had just stared with incomprehension.

In the end I hadn't told the complete truth. I couldn't face confessing that I had suspected Bobby. It was bad enough that he had been beaten up and frightened. I didn't want him to be further hurt and know that I had thought of him as dishonest. The absolute truth was I didn't want him or Jack to know that I had been wrong. I'd said that I wanted to teach Billy Ross a lesson. I pretended that I had naively thought Billy wouldn't look into the bag until he'd driven away. I took the role of a thoughtless girl who had done something that had turned out wrong. It was better to look stupid than devious, better to appear foolhardy than just plain wrong.

'At least Billy Ross won't be bothering us any more,' Jack said, when two policemen led the big man through Casualty. He had marks on his face as though he'd hit something and there was a line of blood across the top of his nose.

'No,' I said, a little hope in my voice. 'Maybe the worst of it is over now. He's been arrested for the hit and run. He's hardly going to say anything to Mickey Duck about the money, is he?'

It was a bad thing to say. Jack gave me a piercing look.

'Trevor Wilkins might die,' he said. 'I don't suppose it'll be much fun spending the money if that happens.'

'Of course, of course,' I said. 'That goes without saying.'

Bobby came out a couple of moments later, followed by his mum. She was talking to one of the other nurses. We walked towards him, me hanging back a bit, trailing the black rucksack behind me. He looked better, his face cleaner and calmer than it had been. Across the top of his nose were two stitches and one of his eyes was puffy and looked as though it would close up. Before Jack could get a word out Bobby spoke.

'I'm finished with the money. I don't want anything more to do with it.'

His voice was like a low whistle, soft but firm.

'Bob—' Jack started to speak.

'I never wanted to be part of this in the first place and now I'm out of it. You two keep it. I won't say anything but it's nothing to do with me any more. Right?'

Jack nodded and I didn't say anything. I caught Bobby's eye for a brief moment and saw a hardness there, his pupils small and dark like bullets.

'You're feeling bad now. I'm not feeling too hot myself. Sleep on it. I'll come and see you tomorrow,' said Jack.

'I'm finished with it!' Bobby said, his hand cutting through the air in a dismissive way.

Mrs Parsons bustled along and took Bobby's elbow. As they walked off I heard a female voice from behind, high-pitched, upset. Chrissie Wilkins had emerged from the treatment area and was crying. I grabbed Jack's arm and tried to hold myself up. Whatever had happened to Trevor was our fault. No – my fault, I knew that. Jack walked towards her, dragging me along.

'How is Trevor?' he said, his voice a little high.

'You found him, didn't you?' she said, taking Jack's arm firmly and pushing him backwards. In a couple of steps the three of us were on the seats, Chrissie Wilkins in between us, each of her tanned hands clasping one of ours.

'Did he say anything? Was he conscious?'

Jack turned to me. I had got to him first. It was me who had looked at his white skin against the dark tarmac lane. I shook my head. Trevor couldn't have spoken to anyone.

'Did the doctors say how he is?' Jack tried again.

'They're going to operate on him.'

This gave me a good feeling. They wouldn't go to all the trouble of operating on the boy if he was going to die. I nodded, willing her to continue, keen to hear more hopeful details.

'He's very weak. The car threw him up in the air and he hit his head on the ground. The doctors say they don't think there's any internal bleeding, maybe not even a fractured skull. He's hard-headed, our

Trevor. His skull's like concrete they say but . . .'

She gave a little hiccup and her hand squeezed my arm. I could feel her nails digging into my skin but I didn't say anything.

'The impact threw him forward and when he came down, on to the road, the car was still going. It ran over him, see. The wheels went over his legs. They're both crushed, bones broken and stuff, but one of them is much worse than the other. That's why they're operating. They may have to amputate it, just above the knee, they said.'

She'd let go of Jack's arm and with her forefinger drew an imaginary line across the top of her knee. I watched her with dismay, my throat feeling parched as though I hadn't drunk water for days.

'He might lose his leg,' she said, her shoulders shaking. She let go of my arm and used the back of her hand to wipe her eyes and her nose.

I didn't have a clue what to say. I felt this weight on my chest, holding me in one position, making it impossible for me to move my shoulders or turn my head. I thought of Trevor, standing across his bike, riding round in ever decreasing circles, always with a bit of gossip, always with a bit of news. I hardly knew the kid really, but now he was tangled up in this mess. He wasn't going to die but he might lose his leg.

We sat like that for a few moments. Then, when a doctor appeared, Chrissie Wilkins leapt up and hurried towards him, her shoes flapping behind her, the strap of her bag twisted up and spinning. She stood in front of him eagerly, fixing her bag with one hand and smoothing her dress with the other, as though her appearance, her poise, might influence whatever it was he had to say to her.

There was nothing else for us to do but go.

When we got back out on to the street it was past eleven. The heat hit us and the weight of the black rucksack was pulling my shoulder down. The sound of thunder overhead promised rain and I could even see several large splashes on the pavement as we walked along.

'What are we going to do?' I said, after a long period of silence had elapsed.

'Wait till tomorrow. Talk to Bobby again. See if I can change his mind.'

Jack's words were clipped, his voice cold. I suddenly felt exhausted; close to tears. I had been upset and frightened by Billy Ross. I had been the first one to find Trevor Wilkins. I hadn't got off scot-free.

'I've said I'm sorry,' I said, with a hint of truculence.

'And that's supposed to make it all right, is it?'

'No, I mean, I know you're angry but . . .'

'Too right, I'm angry. After all we said, about staying together, about acting as a threesome. The first time we agree to do something, you go against it. Bobby could have been badly hurt!'

'I know. I know,' I said, stopping in the middle of the pavement. 'But the thing is I didn't agree. It was you and him. You wanted to give the money over. I never did.'

'So what was the alternative?' Jack stopped walking and turned to me. 'Have Bobby attacked? His house torched?'

'I didn't think it would come to that!' I hissed, the rucksack sliding off my shoulder down towards the ground.

'No, right! You saw Billy Ross – he wasn't exactly playing ring-a-roses.'

'But if we'd all gone together,' I said, looking round the street, trying to keep my voice low, 'he might not have been so keen then.'

'You screwed up,' he said, his finger pointing at me. 'We agreed to act together and you went behind our backs. You got Bobby beaten up and now there's a kid in the hospital who might lose a leg.'

'That's not my fault!' I shouted, pushing his hand out of the way.

I was clenching my teeth, my arms and hands trembling. We stood looking at each other for ten, twenty seconds. It was one thing for me to blame myself for Trevor but I wasn't having anyone else doing it.

'If you'd just left things. If you'd just done as we agreed.'

'I wasn't driving that car,' I said, spitting my words out. 'I didn't run over Trevor. I am not to blame for that.'

'Just everything else!' Jack retorted, turning to walk on.

'It wasn't me who dropped my cash card!' I said, following him, dragging the rucksack along. I'd had enough. I'd said I was sorry. I'd taken the blame but I wasn't going to have my nose rubbed in it.

'You were in charge of the money. You screwed up.'

'I'll tell you what!' I said, raising my voice, tears pricking at my eyes. 'Why don't you take charge of the bloody money? You look after it!'

'I will!' he said.

I dropped the rucksack on the pavement and kicked it in his direction. He didn't move so I turned on my heel and walked away from him. I thrust my hand into my pocket and felt my gran's keys there. Then I started to walk as quickly as I could. I didn't look back. I turned off on a road that led around the perimeter of the park and headed for my gran's. Let him have the money. Let *him* hide it somewhere and worry about it. If Bobby wanted nothing more to do with it then neither did I. It wouldn't take a minute for me get the case out of the loft, then I would march through the dark streets back to Jack's house and give it to him. I had had enough of it.

Above me the thunder sounded louder, over to my left and then moments later over to my right. Great drops of rain plopped down around me and I saw a couple of people up ahead break into a run. I didn't. I kept my pace, holding my face up to the sky and letting the rain hit my skin in cool drops.

Jack could keep the money. It was his decision to take it in the first place. Me and Bobby? We might have nicked a few quid but we'd definitely have left the rest there in Mickey Duck's living-room. If anyone was at fault it was Jack. He'd started it, so let *him* hide it for six months and worry about it.

The rain was heavier, coming down in horizontal lines in front of me, the pitter-patter sound only broken up by a passing car splashing through a sudden puddle. In the streetlights I could see what looked like a sheet of water falling out of the sky, the thunder further away, sounding looser, less angry.

At that moment I seemed to lose purpose, my legs wavering, my feet taking smaller, more haphazard steps. Jack was my boyfriend; my feelings for *him* ran deep. How could I blame him? All I really wanted was to be sitting in the darkness of his bedroom and feel his arms around me and his breath on my skin.

But that wasn't possible because he blamed me for everything. And if I dug the truth out of the deep hole into which I'd buried it I knew he was right.

My gran's house was in view but I had to screw up my eyes to make it out through the downpour. I was soaked by then, my T-shirt sticking to my skin, big damp patches on the thighs of my jeans. I walked on. I would get the money and give it to him. Just to show him that I didn't care about it.

Even though it was late, almost midnight, I could

see lights on in the house next to my gran's. I quickened my pace, getting closer, putting my hand over my eyes to stop the rain, and then I noticed the car parked outside. My mum's car. I stopped for a minute, wondering what had happened. For a moment I thought that the neighbours might have been broken into, and then with a jolt I saw that the lights I had noticed weren't next door, but shining out through the windows of my gran's house, upstairs and downstairs.

I walked on, pushing my wet fringe out of my eyes, going in through Gran's gate. Through the living-room window I could see my mum's shape, moving around the room. I was confused. It was an odd time for her to come to my gran's, even to pick up last-minute things. And then I remembered that afternoon: as I had been coming in the door at home, she had been rushing out. Something to do with Gran, she had said.

A low rumble of fear nagged at me. Was Gran all right? Had anything happened to her? I used my own key and walked into my gran's hallway to hear voices and the words, 'Who's that?'.

I glanced around. Everything seemed all right. Nothing had been disturbed. I walked into the living-room.

'Mum, is everything all right?' I said.

My gran was sitting in her chair, a big smile on her face.

'Course it is, Janice, darling,' she said to me. 'I've

just come home to live in my house again. I told you I would one day, didn't I?'

I looked at my mum, who was standing behind Gran's chair. She shrugged her shoulders, helplessly.

'That's great, Gran,' I said, going over to kiss her cheek.

Then I sat down, wearily, my jeans and T-shirt squelching. It was another plan that had gone wrong. The money would just have to stay where it was.

15

The next day I packed some clothes and my Walkman and moved across the park to live with my gran for a while. She had fallen out with the people at her nursing home. They'd wanted to change her room and put her in a different part of the building and my gran had refused to go. 'I'm not a piece of baggage you can just move around when it pleases you, thank you very much!' She'd barricaded herself in and my mum had been called to sort out the situation. My gran was immovable, though, and after a couple of hours of talking through a crack in the door the supervisor had threatened to get the police involved to evict the old lady completely. This must have given my gran the idea because she struggled to her feet, opened her door and said that she was going home.

My mum had looked relieved when I offered to move in with gran. She gave me a hug.

'Well, if you're sure. It would be a real help,' she said. 'It's just for a while until she gets all the necessary alterations done. I suppose it's not too far for your friends to come, and handy for college. And I'll be over regularly, to check that you're both OK.'

My gran had plans to hire a local firm of builders to

install a shower and toilet in the back dining-room so that she could live downstairs.

'I can't stand that place any more,' she said, referring to the nursing home. 'What's the point in paying them my money? I might as well use it to make myself comfortable here. Then I can look after myself and don't have to have anybody interfering.'

I wasn't staying just because of the money, although some people wouldn't believe this. It was good to see my gran in her own living-room again, holding her TV remote, changing the channels and turning the sound up and down as she pleased. She had only partially recovered from her stroke; her left leg and arm were slow and it was difficult to move around easily. All the same, at home, she seemed to sit up straight in her chair, hold her cup more steadily, eat her food with more control. She talked non-stop about her 'escape' from the home and even made plans for the future. She was going to see a physiotherapist; she was having a walking frame delivered; she was going to get herself a little dog for company, just like Mrs Reynolds, down the road. It was good to be around her.

As soon as I decided to stay it felt right. The sudden distance between myself and Canberra Avenue and the estate was just what I needed. I'd made a mess of everything and didn't particularly want to see anyone for a while. Especially not Bobby (not even Jack, at that point). On the second day, when my mum arrived with a couple of my things and some magazines for Gran, she told me she'd seen Chrissie Wilkins.

'Trevor's surgery went OK. They don't know for sure whether his leg will heal but it's looking quite good. Apparently he's got metal rods sticking out of it and has to stay like that for six weeks or so. That bloke who ran him over? He's been identified by Trevor's little friend. He'll do a fair bit of time for that, your dad says.'

This was a relief. The guilty feelings I had had began to lift and I found myself feeling more relaxed than I had for days. Trevor was all right. Bobby was all right. Billy Ross had been charged by the police and wasn't likely to go shouting his mouth off about the money to anyone.

I gave Gran the toffees I had bought for her ('Janice darling,' she said) and shopped for food for the two of us. I put the cold things into the fridge and felt it rumble a little at the unexpected load before settling back into its usual hum. The whole house seemed to wake up after months of emptiness; the curtains fluttered at the open windows; the rooms smelled of the outside world, the rain, the heat, the scent of a distant barbecue; the hallway echoed with footsteps, the sound of the doorbell and the thud of a daily newspaper dropping on to the floor.

Being with Gran took my mind off things. For the first time in ages I had something else to think about. My insides felt looser, somehow, not so knotted up.

My appetite returned and I even began to think a bit about college. I hadn't forgotten about Jack. How could I? But my feelings towards him were all mixed up with my guilt and embarrassment about the events at the boathouse. I tried to push him to the back of my mind.

My mum and dad moved Gran's bed from upstairs and put it in the corner of the living-room. My mum left her mobile phone next to it so that Gran or I could make contact if we needed to. My dad nailed up a row of hooks so that she could hang some of her clothes on them and they'd found a tiny chest of drawers that she could use. My gran could walk upstairs but it was slow going and she needed someone with her. On the third day I was there a woman from social services came and left a commode. It was an odd-looking chair on wheels that doubled as a toilet. The seat opened up and revealed a bucket. My gran looked aghast at it and said that she wasn't going to do her business in that, 'Thank you very much!', and it was agreed that she would only use it in case of emergency. That was why she got me to ring round local builders and arrange for them to come in and give her an estimate for a shower room and downstairs toilet.

The first company turned up almost immediately. A large florid-faced man filled the hallway. He had an impressive-looking leather belt on which he kept tools hanging like weapons. His mobile phone seemed to be constantly ringing or beeping as I took him upstairs to view the plumbing in the bathroom. I stuttered a bit when he stood looking up at the loft hatch and asked me if the water tank was up there.

It was the one thing I couldn't get away from. The money in the suitcase.

Still, I enjoyed those first days, helping my gran to organize her life, bringing the things she needed from upstairs: her clothes, cushions, pictures, books, even the ballerina jewellery box. She opened it and let the music tinkle while she sorted out bits of jewellery which she hadn't worn for years.

By the fifth day we were in a kind of routine. A woman from the social services called Bev had started to come early in the evening to help Gran have a bath and get ready for bed. Bev checked on her medication and then made sure there was food and everything was all right. By ten o'clock my gran was in bed with the television still on. I sat in her armchair and watched for a while. When she dozed off I took the remote, turned off the set and went upstairs.

Before I went into the spare bedroom I looked up at the loft hatch. Up in the dark, lying on its side, was the suitcase with the money. I had intended to give it all to Jack, to wash my hands of it, but circumstances had delayed that. Now I didn't know what to do.

I went to bed and pictured Jack. I had missed him, there was no doubt about that. Being busy with my gran had meant that I could put off thinking about him. It was as though I had been transported to another world; and the estate, Mickey Duck's money and my secret romance belonged somewhere else. My anger had kept Jack at bay. But I knew that at some point I would have to face up to him and sort out what we were going to do about the money (and us?). It wasn't as if I could blame him for reacting the way he had. I hadn't been honest with him, I'd put everyone in danger.

A wave of regret swept over me and I sat up in bed. I'd been an idiot, I knew that. My suspicions had added up to nothing. It was true that when I recounted the money the amount had been lower, but since then I'd been wondering how accurate the first count had been. We were all buzzing with excitement. Had we made a mistake? If only I had just come clean and shared my worries with them. Wouldn't that have been better? Jack and Bobby had had every right to be furious with me.

I sat cross-legged under my gran's sheets and felt an ardent desire to be with both of them. Bobby and Jack, just slouching round like we used to, maybe sneaking off with Jack somewhere for a kiss and a cuddle. But it was too late for that. In any case, I hadn't been in contact with Jack since the Friday night and for all I knew he was finished with me.

I got up and paced about, wondering what to do. The five days since the events at the boathouse had been a time of denial, that was instantly clear. I had found my gran again and I was feeling safe and warm with my family, but each day made the gap between me and Jack wider. Why hadn't he come to see me? Was he so angry that he couldn't bear the sight of me?

Suddenly I couldn't stand it and I tiptoed downstairs and into the living-room where my gran was sleeping. I picked up my mum's mobile phone from the chest of drawers and took it back upstairs. It took me a minute but I keyed in Jack's number and composed a text message. It was short and to the point. *i miss u cme and c me,* ♥ *jaz.* Then I lay back, listening to the sounds in the street outside, wondering if he would reply.

I must have dozed for a while but the sound of the front gate creaking made me jump awake. I looked at the clock. Less than an hour had passed since I sent the text. Then there was the lightest of knocks on the front door. Ignoring the fact that I was only wearing a T-shirt and a pair of pants I got up and ran downstairs. I could see a silhouette through the glass part of the door and I stopped for a moment, apprehensive of what I had done. I could hear Gran's gentle snores as I walked closer. I knew it was him, something about the shape of his head or the slope of his shoulders. I pulled the door open. The night air hit me, making my skin tingle. I pulled my T-shirt down as far as it would go and blinked into the beam of the streetlight.

Jack was leaning against the side of the porch, taking great gulps of air. He was wearing shorts and a top and trainers with no socks. He smelled of aftershave and tobacco and I stood stupidly, letting my too-short T-shirt flap up so that my pants were on view for anyone to see.

He didn't speak. He just stepped forward into the hallway and put his arms around me. I could feel his heart thumping from where he had been running.

'You're out of shape,' I whispered.

'I must give up smoking,' he said, picking me up and squeezing me tightly.

We went upstairs to the spare room and sat on the bed. Within seconds Jack was kissing me, his mouth searching me out, his hands underneath my T-shirt, his weight pushing me backwards on to the bed until I felt like I was falling, my head thrust into the untidy sheets. Every few minutes he seemed to stop to say, 'Sorry!' and 'I missed you!' and 'Are you all right?'. I found myself moving backwards away from him, fearful of the urgency of his words and his hands, but mostly afraid of what I would do in the dark, in my gran's spare room.

'Wait, wait . . .' I said, breathlessly.

'I've got something,' he said, pulling out a small plastic packet from his shorts pocket.

It was the condom he always had with him.

'I don't know . . .' I said.

But I did know. Every bit of my body was arched towards him, my chest burning and my legs restlessly moving around, not knowing what to do with themselves. It only took a minute for him to get undressed and I let my head drop back on to the pillow as I felt his weight on top of me. I put my arms round him and closed my eyes and let myself be drawn into the darkness, a kind of delicious journey that wiped everything out of my head; all the worries and the guilt just seemed to ripple away as he swooned over my shoulder.

Afterwards we talked for hours. We lay in spoons, him at the back and me curled up in front. I could feel his lips on the back of my neck and I was glad that I couldn't see his face as I told him the whole sorry story. He ummed and tutted and said, 'You silly thing, why didn't you say?' All the while he had both arms round me holding me tight.

'But what about Bobby?' I said, after a while.

'He's out of it. He didn't really want to be involved in the first place. Anyway, he's gone to his cousins' to stay for a while. His mum says he's better off there than with us. She's well hacked off.'

I nodded. Perhaps it would be better if Bobby was out of the way.

'So, it's just you and me?' I said, my thoughts going back to the suitcase in the loft.

'Just the two of us,' he whispered.

And I believed him. How stupid was that.

16

I should explain. There was something different about Jack now.

At first I put it down to the new circumstances we found ourselves in. I spent every day with my gran. Strictly speaking I wasn't actually needed all the time, my gran was OK pottering round by herself, but I liked being there and it kept me away from the estate. The events that had led up to the night at the boathouse had shaken me. Even though I hadn't had any physical injuries I had still been frightened by Tommy Young and Billy Ross. Then there was Trevor, a small boy who had been an innocent casualty of that skirmish by the boathouse. Just thinking about him gave me a nauseous feeling. At my gran's house I felt useful and I could push these things out of my mind.

Jack came round to see me every night. He couldn't make the daytime because his dad had got him some work on a building job that he was doing. He had taken it in order to get some money together before college started. It was important, he said, to have a source of money. It would help to explain some of the things he might buy with the money from the loft.

We both knew the suitcase couldn't stay where it

139

was. Even though we had thrown off Mickey Duck and his friends we couldn't relax, not yet. My gran was back in the house and planning for builders to come in and turn things upside down. It wasn't safe to leave the money in the loft.

Every night, about six, usually while Bev was bathing my gran, I would stand at the front garden gate and watch for Jack coming up the street. I felt like a married woman waiting for her husband to come home from work. He usually had a drink in his hand or a newspaper under his arm, looking years older, a swagger in his step as though he was totally at ease with the world.

My gran loved him. He made an effort and sat talking to her about the sort of things she was interested in. He made her cups of hot, sweet tea and brought in bars of chocolate that she beamed at.

'He's your young man, isn't he Janice?' she said to me one night as I tucked her up in bed.

I gave a secret smile. She was the first person who had noticed the connection between us. It made me feel proud and I thought of all the people whose eyebrows would rise when they knew: my mum and dad, Bobby, my old school friends, people from the estate; even dozy Penny Porter.

We got our exam results. What with everything that had happened it was something that I had completely forgotten about. My mum arrived one morning with the envelope in her hand. When she said, 'Here are your results,' I had to think hard about what she meant. School and exams seemed a lifetime away. My fingers were awkward, pulling apart the envelope on which I had written my own address so many weeks before. I'd taken seven GCSEs. I got four Cs, a B and two Es. I shrugged my shoulders. It was enough for me to go to college and do the course I wanted. So what if my grades weren't inspirational.

'Bobby Parsons got three As and five Bs. One of his As was starred, I think,' my mum said.

'How is he?' I asked, not surprised at his high grades.

'Mrs Parsons said he's coming home from his cousins' tomorrow. I didn't know that you'd all fallen out.'

'We haven't,' I said lightly.

That night Jack was a little late. When he finally walked along the road it was near seven o'clock. He had his mobile phone at his ear and was talking into it. I was keen to know how he had got on in his exams. When he caught sight of me he waved and finished his call.

'I went home to get my results and guess what? Mum and Dad had a bottle of champagne. I couldn't just rush off,' he said. 'Three Bs and four Cs. Pretty good?'

It was only later, when we were sitting having tea and jam tarts with my gran, that I realized that he hadn't asked me what my results had been. My gran told him.

'Janice got lots of Cs, didn't you, love, and an A!'

'No, gran, just a B.'

'That's not bad,' Jack said. 'Well done!'

'I've got to go into college tomorrow for an interview,' I said. 'At ten o'clock.'

'Mine's not till next week,' said Jack.

I felt disappointed. I had imagined us going together.

After a while we left Gran dozing and went up to the spare room. We'd spent a lot of time there since the first night that Jack had come round. Because it wasn't my real bedroom, nor Jack's, and because Gran never went up there, I sort of fantasized that it was our first flat, away from our parents, on our own together.

That night I closed the door and clicked on my cassette player. The window was open and the net curtain was flapping in the breeze. Jack sat down at the head of the bed and pulled his trainers off. I cuddled up beside him putting my arms round his waist.

'I can't come tomorrow night,' he said, lying back on the pillow beside me. 'Dad wants me to go fishing with him.'

It was one of the new things I had begun to notice about him. He seemed to be doing a lot more stuff with his dad. Most nights he talked about the building job he was on, what his dad said, what he said; how his dad made everyone laugh; how, as soon as he was seventeen, his dad was going to teach him to drive and then, if he passed his test, buy him a used car.

He and his dad had always had a good relationship but I didn't remember him being such a topic of conversation before.

'OK,' I said. 'Can't you come round after?'

'It might be an all-nighter,' he said.

Although Jack had visited me every evening he had never stayed overnight. The first night he had left in the early hours but since then he had always left before midnight, mainly because he had to get up for work, he said.

We talked, kissed, cuddled; we even got hot under the collar at times, but we never repeated the sex of the first night. It had been my decision. It wasn't that I hadn't enjoyed it (even though it had all been a bit vague and sticky), it was just that I hadn't wanted it to become something normal, something that was expected from me. Just because our emotions had driven us that far once, I didn't feel I wanted to go there again just yet. In any case I'd promised myself I was going to find out about proper contraception. I'd always been pretty casual about things in life but this was one thing I didn't want to make a mistake about. Jack nodded wisely when I told him all this and shrugged his shoulders good-naturedly.

'If that's what you want, Jaz . . .'

I should have been pleased. Initially I was. But I didn't expect him to lose his passion for me, to stop trying, to hold himself back in the way that he did. We could lie kissing for ages and his hands would stay around my waist. Or if he did push his fingers in between the buttons of my shirt he would pull them back immediately before I'd said a word, saying 'Sorry', as though I had told him off. After a few days I began to think it was a kind of tactic. Because he held back I began to want him more. I moved his hands so that he touched my skin, I arched my head back so that he would kiss my neck and chest. But always he would stop. Then he'd sit up or go over to the chair by the window and smoke a cigarette, letting the fumes drift out into the street.

I was being perverse, I know. I hadn't wanted sex to become a normal thing but I had at least wanted him to put up more of a fight.

He seemed to have undergone a change of heart about the money as well.

'It can't stay in the loft,' he'd said.

'We could find somewhere else, in your house or mine. It could stay there for the six months. That was the original plan.'

'Things have changed,' he said, shaking his head. 'I think we should split it and keep it individually. Once we're at college we can both open bank accounts and start paying it in week by week. No one need know. We can spend it in small ways, things we can use cash for: going out, driving lessons, buying clothes. No one will ever question that.'

'Is it safe though?' I asked.

'Safer than leaving it in that suitcase up there,' he

said, looking up at the ceiling. 'What if some builder found it?'

He was right, I knew. The builders weren't due to start for a week or so but it was probably a good idea to get the suitcase down and put it somewhere else. It was the idea of splitting the money in half that I wasn't happy about. I liked to think of it as *our money*, the two of us together.

That night he started to talk about it again.

'We'll get the suitcase down on Thursday night. We'll divide the money in two. We can both walk back to Canberra Avenue. You put yours in your house and I'll put mine in mine. Then we can come back here, if you want. The whole thing shouldn't take more than an hour or so.'

'Why Thursday?' I said.

I was lying sideways, with my leg over his knees and my arm across him. My hand was under his T-shirt, playing with the fine layer of hairs on his chest. He gave me an absent smile and patted my arm.

'It's probably a good idea to get it out of the way. I'm out fishing tomorrow, so why not Thursday?'

I couldn't think of a good reason. I didn't feel happy about it, though. Mostly I didn't have a clue where I was going to hide my share: I couldn't think of a single place where my mum might not look.

'I think I'll leave mine here,' I said, after a while. 'In this room. I'll be staying here for the next few weeks so it's as good a place as any.'

'Good,' he said, looking pleased.

He sat up suddenly; my arm dropped away and I moved my leg back. He had his back to me and I couldn't help but notice how he glanced down at his watch. It was ten o'clock. He seemed to be leaving earlier and earlier.

'OK if I have a shower? The champagne has made me feel sleepy and it'll wake me up,' he said.

'Sure,' I said.

I immediately relaxed and watched him walk out of the room. How silly I was being. Something was unnerving me, making me unduly critical of him. He'd come round every night, happy to stay in and babysit my ailing gran. He'd been loving and attentive. What more could I ask for?

I heard the shower go on and rolled over, stretching my arms out until my bones cracked. Then I felt something sticking in my back. I turned round and looked into the messy bedclothes and saw Jack's mobile. It must have dropped out of his pocket. I lay back and held it for a moment. Clicking the tiny button I saw that he'd had it on 'Silent' and this pleased me for some stupid reason. He hadn't wanted any phone call to interrupt our time together. I noticed a small envelope icon on the screen. He had a message. I wondered who it was from. Without thinking about it I pressed the button to access the message. In a flash the words came up on the screen. I sat up on the bed and held the mobile under the lamp in order to read them. I had no qualms about it. It was as if Jack's things were mine. I could see no reason on earth why he would mind me reading his text message.

I quickly worked out the abbreviated message, then I read it over once again. As I did I felt my shoulders drop and my throat dry up.

how r u? can't w8 to c u 2nite luv pp

PP. Penny Porter.

I looked over the message again, my mouth open, my lips feeling stretched.

How are you? Can't wait to see you tonight. Love Penny Porter.

For a second I thought, *This is a mistake! Jack's got the wrong message.* But deep down I knew it wasn't. It couldn't have been. It was Jack's phone. It was his message. From the bathroom I heard the water stop abruptly, the sound of the shower curtain swishing back and Jack humming something. He was close, just on the other side of the wall, the tiled room giving his voice some depth. He sounded as though he was enjoying himself. I looked down at the mobile phone and stabbed at the keys to access the text messages he had saved.

One by one they appeared.

mt me 4 a coffee just to chat pp

thnx 4 lst nite can't w8 to do it again pp

thght abt u 2day u alwys were a gr8 kisser pp

It went on, a dozen or more messages. Each one silly and gooey. I could almost picture Penny, the human Barbie, her blonde hair falling in front of her face as she daintily tapped in her messages. I scrolled the messages back until I came to the very first one.

its been a long time lets meet up love penny porter

The date and time were beside it. Almost two weeks before. The day before the three of us went up to the boathouse. The day when Jack was supposedly spending a lot of time with Bobby, to calm him down. The day when I was getting myself wound up about Bobby and his loyalty.

I pressed the button to exit from his saved messages. Then I deleted the one Penny had sent tonight. The screen was blank except for the usual words. The phone sat in my hand, innocent and harmless, just a piece of machinery, and yet it had just ruined everything.

I heard the bathroom door open and a couple of moments later Jack came into the room. He was in his bare feet and looked well scrubbed, his face pink and his hair wet.

'That's better,' he said, smiling.

When I didn't answer he looked a little puzzled.

'You all right?' he said. 'You look upset.'

'I'm fine,' I said, forcing a weak smile on my lips. 'I'm just tired, that's all.'

'I was going to head off anyway,' he said. 'I could do with an early night myself.'

He said it so smoothly. As soon as he closed my gran's door he was going to head for Penny Porter's place. He'd even cleaned himself up for her. He had no trouble at all lying to me.

Some people might say that it served me right.

17

On the way back from my college interview I sat in the back of the car next to my gran. She grabbed my hand with her bony fingers and squeezed. Each day she seemed to get a little stronger.

'Fancy going to college!' she said, her voice hushed with admiration.

'Everyone goes to college now, Gran,' I said, giving her a watery smile.

'You'll do well, you mark my words!' she insisted.

I didn't continue the conversation. I just let her talk on and ummed from time to time. I was sitting in a kind of daze, seesawing from one emotion to another. One minute I was simmering with anger and the next I was puffing with disbelief. Then, inexplicably, I cooled down and felt this welling sadness making my head feel too heavy for my shoulders. In my mind I was replaying the night before and then going over the preceding weeks.

How could I have been so wrong about Jack? It wasn't just our romance (although that was the bit that gave me a *physical* ache); we'd been friends, for years. I thought I could depend on him for anything.

At times during the trip home I had to turn and

stare out of the window, making my eyes as wide as I could. Just one blink was all it needed for me to dissolve into tears. I didn't do it. I'd cried enough the night before.

The college trip had turned into a family outing, my dad and gran sitting on the benches in the grounds of the college while my mum and I went in for the interview. It was quick and easy. The tutor, Celia Abrahams, 'Please call me Celia', was positive about my exam results but mentioned a rather indifferent report I'd got from school which said: *She is sometimes reluctant to engage in work but with the right encouragement and motivation she could achieve higher grades.*

After assuring her that I intended to make a fresh start she gave me a smile and made a lot of notes on a form she was filling in. At the end of the interview she shook my mum's hand and then mine. 'Do ring if you have any problems and ask for Celia,' she said as we left her office and walked back out into the grounds. We found Dad and Gran eating ice creams on the edge of the car park.

When we arrived back at Gran's house she sighed with pleasure. The trip to the college hadn't taken more than an hour and a half and we hadn't driven more than a few miles, but she was acting as though she'd just had a day out at the seaside. Getting out of the car she spotted her neighbour, Mrs Reynolds, and gave her an exaggerated wave. The old lady's dog was jumping up and down, making a racket, and my gran walked shakily towards her. My mum and dad stood awkwardly by the edge of the pavement.

'We'll be off, love,' my mum said. 'Ring me if you need anything.'

For a moment I didn't want them to go. I suddenly felt as if I wanted to say something to them; about the money, the brushes we had had with local criminals, about Trevor and his leg which was full of metal rods, about me and Jack. The words didn't come out, though, and I watched as my mum glanced at her watch and gave my dad a nudge.

'You all right, love?' my dad said. 'You got enough cash?'

He took out his wallet and in a flash handed me a ten-pound note. I wanted to laugh. A ten-pound note when I had thousands of pounds in a case upstairs.

'I'm fine, thanks, Dad,' I said.

'Just call us, if you want a break,' he said.

'I will.'

Mum and Dad said their goodbyes to Gran and drove off. I waved, watching the car disappear up the street, but I don't think either of them waved back. My gran slipped her hand through my arm and we walked up to her front door.

'Your young man came round this morning,' she said.

'What?'

'Mrs Reynolds told me. She said, "Janice's friend was knocking on your door. That lad." She doesn't know that you and him are . . . you know.'

Jack had come round to see me? Why would he? He knew I had the appointment at college. I was thrown by this piece of news. I took my gran into the living-room and settled her in her chair.

'I'll make you some lunch,' I said.

In the kitchen I let my thoughts go where they wanted. Had Jack come round because he realized that I had intercepted his text message? Did he know that I had found out about him and Penny Porter? Was he squirming with embarrassment, ashamed, full of regret?

This thought stopped me. It was something I hadn't considered. Had Jack simply drifted into this relationship with Penny Porter? Was he perhaps regretting it? The past few weeks had been difficult to say the least. We had fallen out, been terse and distant with each other. To top it all I had acted on my own and almost got Bobby and Jack badly hurt. Not to mention poor Trevor. After that I'd withdrawn, spent almost a week away from him. Had Penny Porter been around at a difficult time?

Jack had come round to see me as soon as he got my text message. He'd been eager and keen. I thought of that night on the bed, his long legs tangled up with mine, his weight on top of me, his fingers pressing hungrily into my skin.

Had he got himself stuck with Penny Porter? Was he unable to get away from her? Had he come round this

morning to explain everything, so full of remorse
that he'd forgotten I had to go to the college for an
interview?

I gave my gran her lunch and then took my mum's
mobile phone up to the spare room. I punched his
number in and after a few rings he answered.

'It's me,' I said, controlling my voice, making
it sound unconcerned. 'I wondered why you came
round.'

'Came round?' he said.

From behind I could hear traffic and the sound of
men's voices.

'You came round to my gran's, this morning. I
thought you wanted to see me about something,' I said,
my voice becoming less certain.

'No, I've been at work. Why would I come round?'

'I don't know, no reason, I suppose,' I said, my voice
sticking to the sides of my throat. 'I'll see you later.'

'Remember, I'm going fishing tonight, with my dad.'

'Right.'

I rang off, confused. Why should he deny having
come round to see me? I took the mobile back down
to the living-room and placed it by my gran's bed. She
had finished her lunch and said she wanted a lie down.
I settled her on top of her bed covers and pulled the
curtains across.

'Don't let me sleep too long, Janice,' she said, 'I don't
want to waste the day.'

'I'll bring you a cup of tea about three,' I said.

I went out into the hall and into the kitchen. I had the beginnings of a headache and looked for some painkillers. Then I sat at the kitchen table feeling empty and directionless.

Why would Jack deny coming round to see me?

And then it came to me. Something that had been staring me in the face since the night before. I thought back to those days leading up to the meeting at the boathouse. I had felt distant from Jack. What I hadn't realized was that he had already pulled back from me. He'd spent a lot of time with Bobby. He'd been criticizing my clothes and the way I looked. He hadn't even noticed when I made an effort. When I spent the money that Mickey Duck had given us he'd been angry and dismissive of me.

The days I had spent away from him had simply given him time to cement his relationship with Penny Porter. Why hadn't he just dumped me?

It was an all too easy question to answer. Because I had a suitcase full of money in my gran's loft. Jack hadn't come round this morning to see me. He had no interest in *me*. It was the money he wanted, so he had deliberately come round when he knew I would be out.

This thought made me slump forward, my forehead cradled in my hands. How stupid I had been! Why hadn't I seen it coming? My eyes felt heavy and hard and I had trouble closing the lids. There were no tears, though, just anger, like dry thunder in the back of my head.

I went upstairs immediately. Being as quiet as I could I set up the step ladder and lifted the loft hatch out of the way. I pulled the suitcase out for what I thought was probably the last time. Straining my arms somewhat I carried it down the steps and took it into the spare room. Then I went back and replaced the loft hatch and the ladder.

I counted the money again.

This time it took less than an hour, my fingers and thumbs sore from flicking the corners of the notes. I lay the counted bundles on the bed and checked the total three times. Twenty-seven thousand and eighty pounds. Almost two thousand pounds less than the last time I had counted it and three thousand less than the first total we had reached on the night we took it from Mickey Duck's.

I had blamed it on Bobby. I had imagined him having a key cut to my gran's house and coming back and taking some of the money for himself. Jack had dismissed it. Perhaps we hadn't counted it right on the first night, I'd thought. This time I knew I was right and there was only one conclusion I could draw. Jack had had a key for months. He had taken the money from the suitcase for himself and that morning, while we were out, he had come and taken some more.

I looked at the empty suitcase on the floor and wished, for one moment, that there had never been any money, that I hadn't found it, ticking away like a time bomb in a Nike bag in the corner of Mickey Duck's front room.

I found myself lying on the bed, stretched back across the bundles of money. Some of it was underneath me but other bundles brushed by my face. I picked one of them up, pulled the elastic band off and let the notes fall across my chest. I could smell their oldness, the hands that had coveted them over the years, the perfume that had impregnated them, the tobacco-stained fingers that had peeled them off and passed them on. I felt their toughness, and their wrinkled edges, the folds in them where they'd been fitted into wallets. Some of them I rubbed against my face, twisting and turning on the bed, making a mess of everything, the empty suitcase staring at me uncomprehendingly.

What was I to do?

I lay like that for a while. Then, when things became clearer, I made a decision. I sat up, collecting the ten and twenty-pound notes from the bed. I smoothed them out and placed one on top of the other, making a neat pile. I pulled an elastic band around each pile and put it with the rest.

I went downstairs to make my gran a cup of tea. In the kitchen and living-room I collected a number of things that I needed. Taking the stairs two at a time I ran back up to the spare room, knelt down, and began to pack the suitcase once again.

18

I must have looked odd. It was almost nine o'clock in the evening and virtually dark. There I was, dressed in shorts and a T-shirt, a grim expression on my face, carrying an old-fashioned suitcase. Around my waist I had a bum bag which held a small torch and some matches.

Gran was getting ready for bed. I didn't feel easy about leaving her but she seemed happy enough. I'd shown her the photographs, the ones we'd used to cover the money. She'd been delighted, looking through and pointing out faces from the past.

'Where did you find these?' she said, bristling with pleasure.

'Upstairs,' I replied, vaguely.

When I said I needed to go out for a while she'd been quite happy.

'That's it, spend a bit of time with your friends,' she'd said. 'I've got the mobile phone . . .'

I knew it wouldn't take me long to get up to the lake. I got Gran into bed and checked that she had a drink and some biscuits and that the television remote was beside her.

'I'm all right here, Janice, love,' she said. 'In my own home . . .'

She was looking down at the snaps, absorbed in each one. I closed the front-room door gently, picked up the suitcase from the hallway and left.

As soon as I arrived at the lane that led to the boathouse I got out the torch. I didn't use it straight away because the lights from the main road meant that I could see a fair distance. But when, after a couple of hundred metres, it was too gloomy to see round the bend I switched it on. It threw a faint beam of light ahead and made everything look mysterious. Despite some unease I kept going, up to the point in the lane where we had left Bobby on his own on that night a couple of weeks before. I turned into the bushes and on to the tiny path that led up to the yellow jetty.

I didn't expect to find Jack with his dad, hanging on to the end of a fishing rod. I hadn't come to join in with their fishing expedition.

I crept up through the trees and bushes, pointing the torch into the ground so that I wouldn't alert anyone that I was coming. The suitcase was feeling heavy and a couple of times I stopped to swap it from hand to hand. A rucksack would have been easier but not so dramatic.

I wasn't feeling angry any more. Jack and Penny Porter. Why not? They had been boyfriend and girlfriend in the past. For quite a long time as I remembered. And face it, they were much more suited to each other than Jack and I. Jack had ambitions; he cared about the way he looked; he cared about what other people thought of him. How could I ever have imagined that he would have been happy with me on his arm? Tomboy Jaz, good for a laugh, great fun to hang around with (even nice to roll around a bed with). But to have as a girlfriend? To walk along the street arm in arm?

I had thought that our secret was because of Bobby. We had kept it from him because we didn't want to break up the threesome. Was it like that, though? Had Jack agreed a little too quickly? Did it suit him to tease me and play with me in dark corners, to pretend in front of everyone else, Penny Porter included, that I was just a mate? The money had made it difficult for him to break with me. How could he be sure of what I would do? Especially after the scene with Billy Ross.

Getting closer to the lake I switched off the torch. The bushes were thinning out and I could see the water further up in front. When I got there I stood and looked for a moment. It was absolutely still. There was hardly a sound. The water was as flat as a mirror, the reflection of a veiled moon lying across it. I could see to the opposite bank, to where there were little knots of people fishing, men most likely, lit up by small oil lamps, like stars dotted around the edge of the lake. I turned away and looked at the yellow jetty. It was empty, just a platform of wooden planks that jutted out over the water. On the far side of it I could see a small tent. It belonged to Jack's dad but he was always willing to lend it out. I walked closer, keeping tight to the bushes and holding my breath. I could hear voices bubbling out of the opening.

It wasn't a proper camping tent. It was just big enough to keep the rain and wind (and sun) off two people who were sitting waiting for the fish to bite. This time there were no fishing rods poking out.

I smiled to myself even though my insides felt as though they'd shrunk, my stomach like a tiny balled-up fist. I cleared my throat and then walked up on to the yellow jetty and sat down, cross-legged, with the suitcase at my side. From the tent I heard a deep voice and a silly giggle, and then the sounds of movement, clothes rubbing against the nylon fabric of the groundsheet.

I cleared my throat again. Much louder this time.

From the tent I heard a sharp 'Shush!'. My presence had been felt. I leant across and pressed the catch on the suitcase. It sprung open, making a loud clicking sound. It took a second but the aroma of brandy seemed to rise up and seep out. I breathed it in, a heady, potent smell, courtesy of my gran's drinks cabinet. It reminded me of Christmas pudding and sherry trifle. It was a warm, winter smell and I thought of a crackling open fire and glasses shaped like bells with the honey-coloured liquid swirling round. Not that I liked the taste of it. Too strong by far.

It had gone quiet again so I waited. After what seemed like a long time I heard a scrabbling sound coming from the tent and there was definite movement. I saw feet coming out first and then Jack unfolded himself.

'Hi!' I said. 'I thought I'd join you for the fishing.'

'Jaz?' he said, surprised.

I smiled sweetly and watched as he looked at me and then at the suitcase. He turned back to the tent and mumbled something.

'Tell her to come out,' I said, in a pleasant sort of voice.

A blonde head emerged from the small opening. Penny Porter stood up, stretching her legs. She had a tiny clingy top on with two straps, one of which was hanging down off her shoulder. She was running her fingers through her hair, trying to tidy herself up a bit. It was on the tip of my tongue to say, 'Hey, don't bother on my account.' She looked annoyed, I have to admit.

'Hello Jaz. What you doing here?' she said.

Of course. She thought I was just Jack's mate who had come to interrupt her night of passion. A gooseberry. She really needed to keep better informed. The pair of them were standing about three metres away from me. I decided to get straight to the point.

'Did you tell Penny about us?'

Jack cleared his throat. Penny Porter gave me a look of disbelief.

'Oh Jack,' I said, 'you should have been honest. It's the best policy. You should know that. Look what happened when we weren't honest with Bobby.'

'Can't we talk about this later? When we're on our own?' Jack said it tersely, eyeing the case, not sure why it was sitting there open, some ten and five-pound notes clearly visible. He was too far away to smell the brandy.

'What's going on?' Penny Porter asked, pulling her strap up so that she was properly dressed again.

'It's just that there's something Jack forgot to do. I'm just reminding him. Say the words, Jack. I'm not going to die of a broken heart. *I don't want to see you any more. We're finished. I don't care about you any more. I've met someone new.*'

'Jaz, I can't talk about this here. This is not a good idea. Especially with the . . . the suitcase sitting there.'

'I wondered when you'd notice that.'

I stood up, brushing the dust and dirt from my legs.

'Or maybe you don't want to finish with me?' I said. 'Maybe you want to finish with Penny?'

'What's she on about?' said Penny. 'What's going on? I don't understand.'

Poor Penny was right. She didn't understand. She gave a shrug and turned back to the tent. After a moment she emerged with a tiny rucksack which she hooked over each shoulder. I almost laughed. It was hardly big enough for a doll.

Jack seemed to have forgotten about her. He was looking quizzically at me, his eyes darting towards the case.

'Did you want to say something about the money? Oh yes, I forgot. We're going to divide it in half and keep it in our own houses. Tomorrow night, wasn't it? You couldn't manage it tonight because you were fishing with your dad.'

'Jaz, I know this looks bad but . . .'

'The thing is,' I said, my voice losing some of its strength, 'if you'd just been honest. If you'd just said you'd started up with . . .' I made a hand gesture in Penny Porter's direction. She was standing, looking around, ignoring my presence.

'I was going to tell you but . . .'

'You wanted your money.'

'What money? What's she mean?' Penny Porter said.

'I would have given it to you. Of course I would. You didn't need to take it! To lie about it. I know, Jack, I've counted it. It's nearly three thousand short.'

'Three thousand? I'm completely lost here!' Penny looked from me to Jack.

'Oh shut up for a minute, will you? I can't think,' Jack snapped at her.

Penny Porter stamped her foot and turned and walked back to the tent. She flopped down on the far side of it, her back to the two of us. Jack took a step nearer to me, his eye on the suitcase all the time.

'You took the money, Jack. I told you it was short,' I said calmly.

'I never touched it!'

I opened my bum bag and took out the matches,

careful to keep them covered by my hand.

'You went round my gran's this morning, when you knew I would be out. The money's missing, Jack, I've counted it.'

'You're not thinking straight. Why would I go round and take money when we agreed to split it up tomorrow night? Why would I do that?'

'So you could have more than your share?'

'This is silly. You've just miscalculated. We'll count it tonight and then split it. It doesn't mean you and me are finished. This thing with Penny. It's not serious. It's not like you and me. It just sort of happened. I'll take her home, now. I'll tell her we're finished. Then I'll come round to your gran's and we'll sort it all out. You'll see, when we count it. Nothing's been touched.'

It was tempting. For a brief moment I could see a happy ending. Then I heard Jack's mobile beeping. That insistent prodding sound that told him he had a text message. This time it wasn't from Penny Porter.

But last night it had been.

'This money's been jinxed,' I said. 'It's ruined everything.'

'No it hasn't. You're just tense. We both are. Close the case and take it back to your gran's. I'll come round as soon as I've sorted Penny out.'

His voice was soft and he had a tentative smile on his face. He didn't know if it was all right or not. I took a step in the direction of the suitcase and he took this as a signal that I was going to go along with his plans. He turned to walk back to Penny Porter.

I opened the matches. Standing on the yellow jetty, watching his back as he approached his other girlfriend, I struck the first match and dropped it into the suitcase. Then I struck another and another, walking backwards away from the case, waiting for the fire to take hold.

There was a puffing sound and then a thin flame appeared. It seemed to sway from side to side, looking fragile, as though it might dissolve at any second. But the contents of the case were flammable and a stronger fire burst through from the bottom where the brandy had soaked through. A bright orange light lit up the jetty and the water and the tent that sat on the bank.

Jack spun round.

I stood smiling as he ran back towards the jetty.

'What have you done!'

He was within touching distance of the burning case but he hesitated. His arms were stretched out and for one awful moment I thought he might reach into the flames. He didn't, though. Shielding his face with one hand he grabbed the handle and pulled the case so that it slid off the yellow jetty and on to the earth below. Then he began to kick it in the direction of the lake.

'I'm going home!' Penny Porter said, not moving.

Jack was trying to douse the flames with water. It didn't matter, though. He might find some fragments of ten or five-pound notes but the flames had swallowed up everything else that was there.

'The money was jinxed,' I said. 'We should never have taken it.'

I left him standing ankle deep in water, bent over the suitcase, trying to salvage something. Behind him, his new girlfriend was waiting patiently for attention, her doll's rucksack sitting stupidly on her back.

I'd done what I came to do so I clicked on the torch and walked back into the bushes.

19

I went straight into the living-room as soon as I got back. I was panting even though it didn't seem as though I had run all the way from the lake. I stood still for a moment to calm my breathing. My gran was in bed asleep. She must have dozed off while watching the telly. I picked up the TV remote from her bedside table and turned off the set. I tiptoed round the room tidying up a bit, picking up some of the photographs she'd been looking at from where they'd fallen on to the floor. I took the left over biscuits and drink out to the kitchen. I made a fresh glass of orange squash and took it back into the living-room and put it beside her bed. I did these things mechanically, making myself concentrate and not think about Jack or the suitcase.

Gran looked so peaceful. She had the faintest of smiles on her face. For a moment I envied her. Her life was simple. All she wanted was to be there, in her own home, with nobody telling her what to do. Me? My needs were far more complicated. I made sure her covers were straight, then turned off the bedside lamp and went upstairs.

Once in the spare room I flopped down on the bed and let myself think back over the previous couple of hours. I lay back and felt mildly intoxicated, as though I had drunk some of the brandy, not just used it to start a fire. I kept seeing the flames; an untidy bundle of orange light that had spilt out of the suitcase. Then Jack, his face contorted, trying to grab hold of the handle.

Had I done the right thing?

I felt a moment's sympathy for Jack. He had thought he was going to have enough money to buy a car. Now he had nothing. I wondered what he and Penny Porter were doing at that moment. Was he telling her about the money, explaining how we'd got it, what had happened to us, to Tommy Young, to Bobby and Trevor? Perhaps she was perched on the edge of the yellow jetty, hooking her hair back over her ears, listening to Jack tell the whole story.

I stood up and walked over to the wardrobe. In the bottom, underneath my bag and shoes, was a plastic carrier bag. I squatted down and pulled it out. I took it over to the bed and turned it upside down. The bundles of money fell out and lay in a heap on the bedclothes. How much was left? I wondered. At a guess about twenty-five thousand pounds.

I'd had to use some of the real notes in the suitcase just in case Jack had got too close. If he had stopped me or managed to drench the flames he might have found some fragments of ten or five-pound notes left. It had to be convincing. It was important that he thought all the money was gone. Now all I had to do was hide it again and let some time pass.

Did I feel sad about Jack and Penny Porter? Not at that moment. No doubt, in future weeks, when I saw the pair of them around I would feel upset. I would miss Jack and the way I had felt so comfortable with him. I would miss his warmth and his arms around me. But at that moment I felt a kind of exhilaration. I had faced up to him and taken his money.

Actually, I had done it to all of them. Mickey Duck and his horrible friends. Bobby with his three As (one of them starred) and his snooty mum. Jack and his Barbie doll girlfriend. Me, Jaz, not really very good at anything; average to look at, not much of a dresser, couldn't even keep hold of my boyfriend.

But I had the money and they didn't.

I went into my gran's bedroom and looked around. Her sewing box caught my eye. I placed it on the bed and gently unpacked it. I took out balls of wool and crochet hooks; a box of pins and two pairs of scissors; a dozen or so spools of thread and some swatches of material. I put these things into the top drawer of her bedside chest. I carried the box into the spare room and packed it with the money. It was a tight squeeze but I was just able to close the lid. Then I set up the ladder and took the sewing box up to the loft. It was lighter than the suitcase and easier to hoist up above my head. When I was sure it was far enough away from the opening I pulled the cover over and got down, folding the step ladder back up.

I suddenly felt very tired. It was hardly eleven-thirty but my shoulders and arms felt weary and I was rubbing my eyes as though I had grit in them.

I got ready for bed. I didn't bother to wash or do my teeth, I just put on my nightie and slid between the sheets. Lying there I could smell the forest and the faint whiff of smoke from my hair and skin. I closed my eyes and I could see the lake flat and calm, the suitcase jumping with flames, Jack's face when he realized what I had done.

I must have gone to sleep some time. The next thing I knew it was morning, very early, the sound of birds in the trees but no traffic or people. The light was grey, hardly strong enough to penetrate the curtains. I looked at the clock. The time was six-eleven. I would have liked to turn over and go back to sleep but my mind was busy and my eyes seemed wide open.

I got up, stretching, and went into the bathroom. I turned the shower on and stepped in, washing my hair and scrubbing my skin. Afterwards I took a while to dry off, combing my hair into some sort of style, putting on some clean clothes. It was almost seven before I ventured downstairs. When I peeked into the living-room my gran was still asleep.

I went into the kitchen to make her a cup of tea. While the kettle was boiling I walked into the living-room and opened the curtains, letting the thin morning light stream in. At the top corner of the window was an orange glow where the sun was coming over the rooftops of distant houses. It would probably be another nice day.

I was feeling quite good. I began to plan out the day. Gran and I would go out somewhere. We would get a minicab and go to the shopping centre. They had wheelchairs there. I would put Gran in one of them and we could look around. Later we could find a place to have tea and cakes.

The kettle clicked and I turned round. I was going to make tea for both of us. I intended to bring it in on a tray and set it on the small table. Then I was going to turn breakfast television on and we would watch it and chat about the day ahead.

I didn't move, though. I found myself looking closely at my gran, my eyes narrowing, my chest suddenly hollow, my legs as weak as water.

She was in exactly the same position that she had been in the previous night, the back of her head on the pillow, her face calm, the hint of a smile on her lips. She lay completely still, not a whisper of movement. In the morning light she looked pale, her skin the colour of cement.

'Gran,' I said.

But she couldn't hear me. She was dead.

20

My hand was shaking as I punched the buttons on the telephone. At the same time I found myself backing away from my gran, standing in the furthest corner of the room as though she was something to be afraid of. When my mum answered I couldn't speak so that she had to say, 'Who's there? Who's there?' A couple of times.

'Mum,' I said, hoarsely. 'Mum, Gran's not well. Gran's . . .'

I couldn't say the word. It wouldn't come out of my mouth. *Dead*. It was heavy and final. Like a door closing; a bang and then nothing, just a long silence.

'I'll come over,' she said, quickly, and I heard the call disconnect. There was only the purr of the dialling tone murmuring in my ear. I pressed the '*cut*' button and there was silence and I was alone with my gran – only she wasn't there any more. It was just me.

I took a step closer and found myself standing behind one of the armchairs looking at her still face. How long had she been like that? An hour? A few hours? The whole night? I forced myself to look away and think back. She'd been happy, I was sure. I'd left her lying in bed, looking through her photographs. I gave her some biscuits and a drink and she said goodbye. She had eaten some of them. I was sure. She'd been looking at pictures of her past, friends and relatives, images that she had long forgotten about. I'd taken them from the old brown suitcase and given them to her. She was chatty, flicking through, pointing out people and places to me.

And then she had died. How could that be?

I gripped on to the armchair. If I hadn't gone out I might have noticed something. Possibly she felt unwell, had a headache, some dizziness, some sign that her body was unwell. I let my elbows lean on the back of the chair, my chin pushed into the backs of my hands. I'd not been out long, just over an hour, perhaps a little longer. I'd looked in on her when I returned to make sure she was all right. That was when I'd seen her looking peaceful, the way she was now, her head on the pillow, her face restful. I swallowed back a few times. Was she dead then? Had I been so absorbed with my own problems that I hadn't noticed that all the life had gone from her?

From somewhere out in the street I heard the sound of a car pulling up sharply outside, and then the car door open and slam. I moved away from the chair, my legs feeling shaky, and took a step or two towards the bed. The covers were neat and tidy, as though it had just been made. Had she died some time in the night when I was asleep upstairs? Had she simply taken a last breath and then stopped? Possibly it had been as gentle as that. The life had just eased out of her without even ruffling the bedclothes.

I was by her bed as I heard the front door open and in a second my mum was there, in the room with me, her face drawn, her shoulders rigid with tension.

'Oh no,' she said, a sob hiccupping out of her.

'Mum, I'm sorry,' I said.

But the room blurred up and I closed my eyes, sending tears down the sides of my face. Poor Gran. She'd only just escaped from the nursing home and she was full of plans and now it was over. I could hear my mum crying and then I felt her arms around me, squeezing my chest so tightly I could hardly breathe.

'Poor Gran,' I said.

As soon as the ambulance crew had taken Gran's body away my mum pulled herself together and became business-like. She told me to pack my stuff and said that she was taking me home. I did. By midday I was back in my own bedroom and I could hear my dad on the phone downstairs making call after call, telling people that Gran had gone.

Mum and Dad were full of sympathy and kept reassuring me that Gran hadn't died because I hadn't been there to look after her. The doctor at the hospital phoned to say that he thought she'd died of heart failure some time the previous evening. This was not unexpected for someone with her medical history.

Nobody blamed me but I wanted to tell them the whole truth, to explain why I hadn't been there; to stand in front of them and upend the black plastic bag of money. 'This was what I thought was important!', I wanted to say, but it would have changed nothing. Even if I had been there, watching television beside her, I couldn't have done anything to keep her alive. Instead I made up a story about me going to the shop on the corner to get some crisps and sweets. When I got back, I said, she looked as though she was asleep so I turned the television off and went to bed myself. Anyone could have made that mistake, Mum had said. She was adamant that I had done my best.

Unpacking my bag I found some of the photographs that Gran had been looking at. For some reason I'd taken them with me. I sat cross-legged on my bed and laid them out in front of me as though they were playing cards. Six colour pictures of people that gran knew when she was much younger; at the seaside, in front of a church, in a park. The people were all smiling, looking at the camera. Gran herself was in a couple of them. She had been thrilled when I gave them to her and was looking at them before she went to sleep. They were her last views of life.

To me they had been useful for covering up the money.

I turned to the side and lay down, pulling my knees up to my chest. I thought of Jack and Bobby: two friends who didn't like me any more. How could I blame them? I didn't like myself much either.

21

The funeral was to be the following Friday, the last day of the long summer holidays. My mum and dad had decided that it would start and end at Gran's house, so we went round there a couple of times during that week to give it a good clean and get it ready for the mourners to come back and have refreshments after the ceremony. I cleaned the kitchen while Mum and Dad did the living-room and took gran's bed back upstairs. I scrubbed the worktops and cleaned out the fridge. I wiped over the unit doors and swept and washed the floor. I rinsed the sink, pouring bleach down the plughole, and wiped the tiles until they shone. I wanted the place to be spotless.

When I was finished I stood and looked at it with satisfaction. Gran always liked everything to be spick-and-span.

'What'll happen to Gran's house?' I said, as we got ready to leave.

'It'll probably come to me. She won't have made a will. You know how she hated anything official. We'll have to wait and see,' my mum said.

I quite forgot about the money in those few days. I knew it was up in the loft, but that knowledge was in a shadowy part of my mind and I only glimpsed it from time to time. Moving back home had been odd. Even though I'd only been gone a couple of weeks everything seemed different. My house looked bigger, huge in comparison to Gran's. It was full of sounds that I wasn't used to: the shower running, the vacuum cleaner, the washing machine rumbling away down in the kitchen. My bedroom had been tidied and Mum had bought me some new curtains and matching duvet cover. She bought a new shoe tidy for me. It hung in my wardrobe and had lots of little compartments for me to slot my trainers and sandals into. I sat looking at it for ages, marvelling at how neat it all looked. At the bottom, in a pile, was my old school uniform. It looked as though my mum had washed and ironed it. I took it out and held it up against myself. It looked ridiculously small, as though I had grown over the summer.

Mum tried to keep busy and included me in almost everything she did. I was grateful. Having a lot to do made time pass quickly. It meant that the events of the last few weeks were fast receding into the past. It was like travelling in a fast car away from some unhappy place.

We went shopping. My mum bought some black trousers and a top for the funeral as well as a tie for my dad. Then she took me round the shops and bought me some clothes for college: jeans, shirts, a couple of skirts and some proper leather shoes.

'You could wear those to the funeral,' she said, when I tried it all on at home. 'Your gran always liked to see you dressed up.'

She also bought me a bag for my books, a new pencil case with pens and highlighters and a pad of lined paper.

It was all small stuff, the new clothes, the duvet cover and shoe tidy, the highlighter pens and stationery, but it made everything feel different. As though I was moving on to a new bit of my life and starting afresh. Most of the time this pleased me. Only now and then, when I was on my own in my bedroom, did I feel that things were going too fast; that as well as leaving the events of the past few weeks behind I was also moving away from my gran – that she wasn't just in some nursing home up the road and I would never see her again. That's when I slammed my wardrobe door and kicked my trainers into the middle of the floor. I screwed up my new college clothes and swept my stationery off the bed. Because what did any of it matter? The past? The future? The money in the loft? I sat on the floor of my room and played with Gran's keys; a Chubb and a Yale and the letter K for Katherine. Then in a moment of temper I threw them at the wastepaper bin, only to pick them up again ten minutes later and put them back in my drawer with her photographs.

I hadn't seen Jack at all. In all the trips up and down Canberra Avenue, in and out of the house, back and forth to the car, up to the precinct and back, there had been no sign of him or Penny Porter. I knew he was probably still working with his dad but I expected to see him around in the late afternoon or evening, or maybe just out in the street. I half hoped he would come to the house to say something about Gran. He had liked her, too, but he was most probably avoiding me, I thought.

I did see Mickey Duck.

He was in his car as I passed, a couple of odd-looking lads hanging around him. Then, when I was coming out of the shop in the precinct, he was standing talking to a man with a shaved head who I had never seen before. He was wearing a light-coloured suit that had a sheen on it and he seemed to be looking past his friend at his own reflection in the shop window. He nodded to me, in an absent-minded kind of way, as though he knew me but wasn't quiet sure from where.

I'd heard that Billy Ross had been refused bail and was awaiting trial for the hit and run. I don't suppose he would have come back to the estate anyway, seeing as there was a lot of bad feeling about Trevor Wilkins.

The other person I saw a couple of times was Bobby Parsons. Looking out of the car window I spotted him going into his house. Then, when I was walking up to the paper shop, he came out of his gate. He stopped for a moment as though he was going to say something. Then he just nodded and walked on. I felt this stab of remorse. I hadn't treated him well at all. I found myself looking out of my mum's bedroom window in the direction of his house to see if he was coming out. I asked my mum if she'd seen Mrs Parsons, hoping to get some information about what he was doing. I began to think about him a lot and the funny thing was I didn't just think of *Bobby*. Whenever he came into my head I thought of him as *Bobby* Parsons. It was like he had become a different person as well.

On the day of the funeral I woke early. I got the clothes out that I was going to wear and I laid them on my bed. Dressed in old jeans and a T-shirt I went downstairs and made myself some breakfast. I could hear Mum and Dad pottering around upstairs, the bathroom door opening and shutting, the flush of the toilet, the sound of the television from their bedroom.

I sat there nursing a mug of tea and I suddenly felt dreadfully alone. Both my friends had gone and my gran was dead. Upstairs I had a bedroom full of new things and in my gran's house I had a box full of money. But I was on my own, with no one to talk to, no person to confide in or share jokes with.

I got up and found myself walking towards the front door. It was only eight o'clock but I thought I might just catch Jack. I had this extraordinary idea. What if he saw me, there in front of him? What if I told him about the money? What if I explained how angry I had been and how much I missed him? Would he forgive me? How serious was this thing with Penny

Porter anyway? He and I had been together for *months*. I quickened my pace as I went out of the front door. Why shouldn't we get back together? A wave of optimism swept me along the pavement and for a few seconds I felt hopeful.

Jack's mum answered the door.

'Oh Jaz, it's so nice to see you. I heard about your gran. I'm really sorry, I know you were close to her.'

'Is Jack in?' I said.

'No . . . He's staying over at Penny's.'

Somehow, I kept a smile on my face.

'He'll be back later, though. At least he says he will.'

'Does Jack know about my gran?' I said.

'Yes, hasn't he said anything to you? That's boys for you. They can't deal with feelings!'

'Yeah,' I said.

'Tell your mum we'll be thinking of her. I hope the funeral goes well.'

I walked away, my legs like jelly. How stupid of me, how silly I was. Of course Jack was with her. How could he not choose her over me? I had thrown away all his money. How could he ever bear to look at me again?

I wasn't looking where I was going and I almost bumped into Mrs Parsons, who was striding along the pavement. She stopped for a moment.

'I'm sorry about your grandmother, Janice.' She said it in a clipped way as though it was something she thought she ought to say.

I watched as she disappeared round the corner and

thought about Bobby Parsons. I could go to see him. I could tell him everything, confess, offer to share the money with him. Split it two ways. Why not? It wasn't as if I hadn't been thinking about him over the past few days. I had felt awful about what had happened. Perhaps if I hadn't had that row with Jack I might have gone to see him and made things right again. In some ways the whole situation had been caused by Jack anyway. He had been the one who had persuaded us to take the money. Bobby Parsons and myself had had nothing but trouble since that day. Why shouldn't he and I share it? Why couldn't we make it right, now, at this last minute?

Bobby answered his front door almost as soon as I rang the bell. He looked taller or something. His bruises had gone and he was wearing a shirt and trousers that I had never seen before.

'Can I come in?' I said.

He stood back without saying anything. I walked past him and stood awkwardly in the hall.

'What do you want?' he asked. His voice was frosty and he stood stiffly.

'Did you hear about my gran?' I said.

He nodded, his voice a little softer. 'Yeah. I was sorry. I know you got on well with her.'

'Look, I need to say some things to you. Tell you some stuff. Mostly I need to say sorry.'

I couldn't read his expression. He gestured for me to go upstairs and I walked up quickly, my spirits rising.

He was taking me up to his bedroom just like he had in the days when we were real friends. I walked into the room ahead of him and, as usual, found it in pristine order, the bed made, the window open, letting the warm summer air into the room.

His computer was on, the screensaver building crazy puzzles in bright red and lime green. Beside it, on the desk, I noticed what looked like a new colour printer. His mum was obviously getting him ready for college.

'Sit down,' he said, pointing to the chair by the window.

'I should start by telling you about me and Jack,' I said, when he'd settled himself on the bed opposite me. 'You see, a couple of months ago . . .'

'You don't need to tell me about that. Surely you didn't think that I didn't know?'

I felt foolish.

'The two of you were all over each other. I couldn't go out of the room without the pair of you snogging or groping each other. I'm not blind.'

'We meant to tell you but just didn't get round to it.' I held my hands out, trying to explain.

I went on, describing my anxieties about the lack of honesty between the three of us.

All the while he sat looking at me. From time to time he brushed something off his trousers, or looked at his fingernails or fiddled with the collar of his shirt. Although I was sitting in his bedroom as I had done a hundred times before, I didn't feel comfortable. I had expected him to be shocked, angry, upset, but ultimately pleased that I was there. He didn't seem to be going through any of these emotions.

'It was wrong. We should have been honest, I know that now.' I was selecting each word carefully, hoping that one of them would trigger a reaction from Bobby Parsons. Instead each word seemed like an invisible brick building a wall between us. When I got to the part about my suspicions about the money I decided to be brutally honest. I had nothing to lose.

'I thought you had had a key cut to my gran's and had nicked some of the money. That's why when you said Billy Ross had been to see you I didn't believe it. I thought you were trying to trick us out of our share. I'm so sorry. I've never been so wrong about anything. It wasn't you at all. It was Jack. I'd trusted him and he let me down . . .'

The words were flowing, gushing out. I felt lighter, easier. I'd held all these things in for too long.

Bobby was shaking his head.

'I know it's hard to believe. Jack let me down. Not just with the money but with Penny . . .'

He made a dismissive gesture as though he didn't believe it.

'Honestly. My gran's neighbour saw him coming round when we were all out. I counted the money and it was a couple of thousand short. He denied it. But someone saw him. He lied about it. Just like he lied about Penny Porter.'

'I don't know about Penny Porter,' Bobby Parsons replied at last. 'That's Jack's business. I do know that he didn't take the money.'

'But . . .'

He stood up and put his finger over his lips. The gesture immediately irked me. It was absolutely classic and reminded me of Jack, the sort of thing he might do. I was tired of people bossing me. I kept my irritation inside, though, and got up to follow him over to his desk.

'I've been meaning to return something to you. There, in the top drawer.'

Puzzled, I pulled the drawer open. It was empty except for a key-ring with two keys on it. A Chubb and a Yale. I looked at him and the penny finally dropped. They were the keys to my gran's house.

'I don't understand.'

'I don't see why. You and Jack kept something from me. I kept something from you. I didn't intend to take the money. I only had the keys cut so that I could keep an eye on things. But when I went to check I thought, why not? Why not hide something from them?'

'But you could have had a third of it. After that night with Billy Ross you said you didn't want any!'

'I didn't want to be part of any little *arrangement* with either of you. Then, when I got back from my cousins' a couple of days ago, I thought, why should they have it all? My mum said you were staying at your gran's. When you weren't in I thought, why not go in and take a couple of thousand?'

'But I would have given it to you . . .'

'It was never yours to give, and anyway, I didn't want to have to be grateful to you. I wanted to take it. I could have taken it all but I'm not that bothered. I just thought I deserved something.'

I fiddled with my hair, not knowing what to say.

'Here!'

He threw the keys at me. I tried to catch them but they fell through my hands. I picked them up off the floor and turned to go. From behind I heard him speak.

'I hope the funeral goes well.'

My mum was at the gate when I got back. She had her black clothes on and was looking agitated.

'Where have you been? We've got to set off in fifteen minutes!'

I didn't answer. I just ran up the stairs, into my room and slammed the door as loudly and viciously as I could.

22

After the funeral the black limousine drove us back to Gran's house. The cars that followed parked along the street and several relatives and old family friends came for a last visit. There were sandwiches and cakes and tea and coffee. For those who felt like it there was sherry and spirits. Some of the neighbours came along and within a short time the house was full of chatter. My mum, who was tearful at times, seemed generally composed and in charge of things.

I had gone through the church service in a kind of daze. Instead of thinking of Gran I kept poring over the events of the preceding few weeks. How stupid I had been. How quick I had been to misread everything, trusting the wrong person at the wrong time. Instead of listening to the vicar when he was talking about my gran's life I was thinking about Bobby and Jack – both of whom had let me down – my face twisted with anguish. Some people might have thought I was trying to stop myself crying but the truth was I was trying to stop myself from exploding with frustration.

And then, in a quiet moment, I looked up at my gran's coffin, sitting peacefully at the front of the church. On top of it was a simple wreath of pink roses. I remembered her words, when she was looking at the photographs: 'I'm all right . . . here in my own home,' and I suddenly felt empty and light-headed as though a puff of wind would blow me away. Gran was gone and I was thinking about myself. How absolutely typical.

Back at the house, feeling calmer, I carried the plates of sandwiches round. I chatted to Gran's neighbours and some of her old friends from the Bowling Club. My mum was in the middle of a small circle of distant relatives and I could hear snatches of what she was saying.

'Mum didn't have solicitors. She was very suspicious of officialdom . . .'

'She was feisty. That's why she didn't get on in that nursing home . . .'

'She didn't leave a will. You know what she was like. At least I haven't found anything, yet . . .'

As people left I took cups and plates out to the kitchen. My dad was washing up and I heard him talking to some thin, white-haired man about his car and how he was going to sell it and buy a better model.

The morning was slipping into the afternoon. Bobby Parsons' words seemed a long time ago. I went upstairs to the toilet and passed under the loft hatch. The money was still there and when all was said and done I still had twenty-seven thousand pounds to myself. It should have raised my spirits. I didn't have Jack any more and my friendship with Bobby was definitely in the past, but I was starting college on the following Tuesday and I would be able to meet new people. The money could buy a lot of things. So why didn't I feel better about it? I shrugged and went into the bathroom, closing the door tightly behind me.

I stayed up there for a while, hearing the front door opening and closing and several people saying goodbye. When I finally went back downstairs there were only a few people left and they were standing up, picking up bags, patting their pockets for keys, saying their farewells.

'Janice, love, would you walk Mrs Reynolds to her door?' my mum said, rolling up the sleeves of her blouse.

'Sure,' I said, taking the old lady's arm.

I left my mum and dad virtually alone, starting the general clear-up. Mrs Reynolds was full of conversation.

'Your gran was always talking about you,' she said, as we edged slowly along the pavement towards her house.

'I'll miss her,' I said, meaning it.

'She said you had a young man!' Mrs Reynolds went on.

'Not any more,' I said, making an exaggerated face to show how upset I was.

'Never mind, dear. Plenty more fish in the sea. What about that other nice boy? The dark-haired one that I saw last week?'

She meant Bobby Parsons. At the time, when my gran had told me, I had jumped to conclusions and thought she meant Jack. I shook my head. It was too late to do anything about any of it.

Mrs Reynolds' dog jumped up at both of us, barking and wagging its tail furiously. I squatted down and stroked it while the old lady chattered on about her grandchildren. Then she insisted on walking me round her living-room and showing me pictures of all of them. With each one I got an explanation and a quick résumé of their achievements at school or dance class or whichever musical instrument they were learning. Eventually, after declining several offers of tea or lemonade, I said my goodbyes.

Closing Mrs Reynolds' front door I looked up and saw Jack across the street, leaning against the garden wall of the house opposite. The sight of him startled me and I stood completely still. After a couple of moments I pulled myself together and walked out of the front gate. I must have looked calm and unconcerned but I could feel my heart banging and my blood racing through my veins. He stood up straight, looked both ways along the road and crossed towards me. I brushed down my skirt, feeling embarrassed and exposed.

'You look nice,' he said, pointing to my clothes.

He was wearing pale-coloured trousers and a short-sleeved shirt. In his hand he had an unopened pack of ten cigarettes which he was playing with, turning it over, sliding it between his fingers, moving it from one hand to the other.

'I'm sorry about your gran. She was a sweet old lady. I liked her.'

I nodded, still not sure why he was there, what he wanted. He seemed to read my mind.

'I came to see why you called at my house this morning.'

What could I say? How could I explain the carousel of emotions I'd been on all day? I hung my head and he moved a step closer and put his hand on my arm.

'I don't care about the money any more. I've been an idiot, I know that. Me and Penny? It was just passing time.'

I avoided looking directly at him. Instead I glanced down at my shoes, turned to see the flowers in the nearby garden, watched a van that was unloading some paving slabs along the way. Inside my emotions were in freefall. Finally I settled my gaze on the pack of ten unopened cigarettes.

'Trying to give up again?' I said.

'Yep.'

More than anything I wanted to put my arms out and pull him towards me. How simple it would have been. To forget everything that had happened and start again. The gap between us was tiny, a few centimetres. It seemed much further, though, and I wasn't sure if I could make the leap.

'Tell you what,' he said, sensing my reluctance. 'Let's

not say anything now. Why don't you come round to my house tonight? We can talk about it. See what happens. Start again.'

'What about Penny?' I said.

'History.'

He said it with certainty and I felt this rush of hope in my chest. He raised his hand and ruffled my hair. Then he turned and walked off, throwing the cigarette packet in the air and catching it again. I watched him go with a sense of wonder. Could it really be as simple as that? I thought. Could we get back together after all that had been done?

Then I remembered the money. Still there, most of it, packed neatly into an old lady's sewing box, just waiting to be taken away. Could the whole sorry mess end this way? Me and Jack back together, the money split and put into two bank accounts?

Why not? Bobby had taken all he wanted and had made it clear that he wasn't interested in being friends. Why shouldn't Jack and I have the rest?

I almost skipped back to the house. I had to stop myself from humming a tune, to pull myself back from the delight I was feeling. It was the day of my gran's funeral but everything had changed again. There was a chance to put things right, to go back to the way it used to be. The front door was shut and I didn't have my key so I rang the bell. There was no answer but I hardly noticed at first, I was still miles away, thoughts of me and Jack and our future ringing round my head.

I pressed the bell again, a couple of times. It was odd. I put my finger on the bell and left it there, impatience building up inside me. When there was no sound of anyone approaching the door I was puzzled. I turned round and saw my mum and dad's car so I knew they hadn't gone out. It occurred to me that they'd gone into gran's back garden and couldn't hear the bell, so I pressed it again, for a long time, the chimes sounding musical and insistent. I also banged on the glass and called out, hoping they would hear me. A woman walking her dog gave me a funny look as she passed.

I was beginning to get annoyed when I heard my dad's voice in the distance. At last! I relaxed and heard footsteps coming down the stairs and then the front door was flung open.

My dad stood there. He'd taken his suit jacket and tie off and rolled up the sleeves of his shirt. He seemed breathless and looked strange, as though he'd just been cleaning the car. His face was shining with perspiration and his hands and arms were covered in dust.

'What took you so long?' I said.

He didn't speak but I heard my mum's voice from upstairs.

'Janice! Come up here. Quick.'

I stepped into the hallway and looked up the stairs. From where I was standing I could see the step ladder. An awful feeling took hold of me; I seemed to sway and had to put out my hand and steady myself on the wall. My dad rushed past me and was up the stairs in an instant.

'Janice, look. You won't believe it! I've found something of Gran's.'

I could see my mum squatting down on the landing, bending over something. My dad was kneeling beside her, his face lit up. I couldn't move. I felt this dragging sensation as though the bottom half of me was suddenly heavier.

'Come on. Come and see what Gran left!'

After a moment I started to walk up towards them. I took each step slowly, feeling out the stair before putting my weight down. My hand was resting on the banister. It was as though I was actually walking behind my gran, waiting for ages for her to negotiate each step, reassuring her that it didn't matter, that I wasn't in a hurry and she could take all the time that she wanted.

I was halfway up and could see the gaping loft hatch, the cover pushed aside, just a dark hole, like the opening to a cave.

'Look at this!'

I could hear the awe in my mum's voice and by then I was close enough to see my parents, the sewing box between them, its lid flung back and some of the bundles of money out on the floor.

'It's all in small notes. Tens and fives. Your mum must have taken years to save it.'

'I told you she didn't trust banks. I knew she was careful but I never thought . . .'

When I got to the top they both looked round.

'We were just having a look around for Gran's papers. Your dad poked his head in the loft and look what he found! It must have been up there for a good while.'

'Since before Gran had her stroke,' my dad said, holding a bundle of money in each hand.

'She must have forgotten about it! Otherwise she might have said . . .'

'No, you know what she was like. She didn't like anyone knowing her business.'

'There's thousands of pounds here! Maybe twenty thousand.'

Twenty-seven thousand and eighty pounds, I wanted to say.

'We'll have to put it straight into a bank account. We don't need to say anything about it to solicitors and stuff. You never know whether the Inland Revenue might want some of it,' my mum said, breathlessly.

'Janice won't say anything, will you love?' my dad said, giving me the quickest of looks and then returning to the money.

'Course she won't. And don't think you won't get something out of this, Janice. Your gran would have wanted that.'

I left them on the top landing, chattering gleefully, and went downstairs to finish the tidying up. I dried the remaining dishes and put them into the cupboards. I tipped out the last of the milk and washed the sink.

I turned the fridge off at the socket and wedged the door open. I locked the windows and the back door and waited on the bottom stair as my mum and dad came down with the money in an old shopping bag of Gran's.

'We're going to take this home tonight and bank it in the morning,' my mum said. 'It's what Mum would have wanted.'

I found myself laughing, just a little at first then a lot, as if I had just got the punch line of some very funny joke. After a few seconds the laughs turned to tears, silent sobs that kept coming even though I tried to restrain them.

'What's up?' asked my dad.

'It's delayed shock. About Gran. I understand, Janice. We all have our own way of grieving.'

They took me home and I stayed up in my room for the rest of the evening. I didn't go to see Jack. I had nothing to say to him.

23

The following Friday, about nine o'clock, I found myself walking towards the precinct. It was dark and there was just a hint of autumn in the air. I was still wearing short sleeves but every now and then I felt the need to rub my hands up and down my arms to warm them up.

I had just finished my first week at college. I had a full timetable and a bag stuffed with homework. I had a new bus pass and an identity card that enabled me to use the library and the IT rooms. The place was huge, with more than two thousand full-time and five thousand part-time students. It took me almost fifteen minutes to walk from one end of the site to the other. I felt like a tiny fish in a big sea. Luckily I'd latched on to some kids from my old school. A couple of girls who had left the previous year were in the same tutor group as me and we sat together at lunchtime. I'd seen Bobby only once, from a distance, and passed Jack in the cafeteria a couple of times. We hadn't spoken.

I went into the shop and bought a cold can of Coke. I paid for it with a ten-pound note and the shopkeeper had a moan about not having enough change. Then I went outside and sat on a low brick wall and took gulps of the fizzy drink. There were several people around, mostly younger kids and a few from my old school. I pushed my change into my pocket and felt the other ten-pound notes sitting there.

It was the remains of the hundred pounds that my mum and dad had given me out of 'Gran's money'. I had shown gratitude even though I had felt like throwing it back at them. Then I thought, why blame them? None of it was their fault. They were like two kids who had happened on an unexpected bag of sweets. So I had some money to spend for my first week at college. My mum had suggested that I open a bank account but I didn't bother. It wasn't going to last long.

A car pulled up along the way and Chrissie Wilkins got out, slamming the door loudly behind her. She shouted something back into the car and then walked rapidly towards the shops. She had shorts and a strappy top on and looked as though she'd just come from a sunshine holiday. I looked back to the car and saw the shape of a head in the passenger seat. I had a feeling it was Trevor, strapped into the seat, his leg peppered with steel rods, no gossip to report. Chrissie dashed past me and towards the chip shop, barely giving me a look, probably too preoccupied with what she was doing to remember who I was. She opened and closed the door and the aroma of frying food and vinegar wafted out on to the pavement, making me feel suddenly hungry.

In the distance I saw a shape coming towards us and I thought, for a moment, that it might be Jack. I waited for him to get closer and then realized that it wasn't him, just some other tall, thin, young boy walking with a swagger. As he passed by he threw me a glance and straightened up as though he knew I was watching him. I smiled to myself. He thought I had eyes for him. He didn't know that I was only measuring him up to someone else.

I could have gone back with Jack. I knew that. But when all was said and done he had chosen someone else over me and that was something I would not be able to forget. And Bobby? On my way to the precinct I had passed his house and looked up briefly at the 'FOR SALE' sign. Bobby was moving to the other side of London – twenty-eight stops on the Central line.

Chrissie Wilkins ran past me again, clutching her fish and chips. Behind me were some kids on bikes, not much older than Trevor. I could hear them talking excitedly to each other. There was a fight, outside the Queen Mary pub. Some young men were squaring up to each other. There were drugs involved and some of them had brought knives. The police were on their way and there were bound to be arrests. They were whispering loudly, their voices tense with anticipation. One by one they cycled off up the road, looking forward to some drama, anything to brighten up a dull evening outside the chip shop.

Me? I finished my drink and walked through the dark streets towards home. I was too old for all that kids' stuff.

INNOCENT

Charlie is well acquainted with the police. Her brother Brad is constantly in trouble. But this time it's serious. A man is dead and Brad is in the frame for his murder. Something about the crime doesn't add up, though. Charlie is convinced Brad is hiding something – or someone.

But in trying to prove her brother's innocence, is Charlie letting go of her own.

CARELESS

Nicky Nelson and Chloe Cozens could be brother and sister . . . except they've never met. Until now. Chloe's mum was important to Nicky, she believed in him. But he wasn't her flesh and blood. And now Nicky resents Chloe for being what he never was.

But when he meets Chloe, he has to change his mind. Chloe knows Nicky is dangerous – damaged – but she's kind and she seems to understand him . . . Just like her mum did. But can even Chloe help Nicky find what he's been searching for all his life?

THE DEAD HOUSE

Lauren Ashe is coming back to London from Cornwall to start college; she'll be staying just streets away from the house where she lived as a little girl, with her mum, dad and little sister . . . It should bring back happy memories, but for Lauren, going to see her old house just brings back nightmares.

Lauren knows she has to face up to the past, she has to find out the truth about what happened to her mum and her sister – and her dad. And the truth lies closer to home than she thinks . . .